HOOD WIVES & RICH THUGS OF MIAMI 2

SHYKEL W.
LA'QUANA JONES

Cole Hart
SIGNATURE NOVELS

Mailing List

To stay up to date on new releases, plus get information on contests, sneak peeks, and more,

Go To The Website Below...

www.colehartsignature.com

"There's no way that we can work it out... If we don't pull together... I don't mean to be demanding... I want some understanding... I want to be with you." Amber sang her heart out as she pulled into her drive way.

The lyrics of Understanding by Xscape spoke volumes to Amber's heart. Unfortunately, she was able to relate to the song in many ways that she wished she didn't. Just like the lyrics, Amber was the only one attempting to work on her marriage, and Jamison wasn't trying to help in any way.

"Best fiendddddddd!"

"Daisyyyyyy!" Amber yelled in excitement upon hearing her best friend.

"What the hell are you doing? I miss you."

"I miss you as well. I'm just pulling up to my house from work."

"Good timing. Are you still going out with us tonight?" Daisy asked.

"Of course, I am. I already have my babysitter booked and ready for drop off," Amber said through her smile.

"Yes bitch, yes. I love my god daughter and all, but we need this girl's night."

"Hell yea, we do. How long will you be in town this time?"

"Two short ass weeks." Daisy answered after taking a deep sigh. Daisy moved to New York to pursue her modeling career. Amber wished her best friend nothing but the best and wanted to see her succeed, but at the same time she missed having her around.

"Awe damn, we have to make the best of the weeks than."

"You know good and well, I already have everything planned out and reserved."

"Good."

"Mo told me some shit about Jamison breathing down the back of our neck, what's going on with that?" Daisy inquired.

"Chile, he been out doing all his dirt and now that he thinks I'm doing the same. So, now he wants to stay home and be all under me, as if it will make things better."

"So, is he being dragged along tonight?"

Daisy was no fan of Jamison and the way he treated her best friend. Out of respect for her sister, she tolerated him. However, that didn't stop her from voicing her opinion. Even though it all fell on deaf ears, Daisy knew that eventually Amber would see the light at the end of the tunnel.

"Hell no. Shit, I need some space away from his ass. I be ready when he get back to doing whatever it was that he was doing."

"Amber, don't say things you don't really mean." Daisy said as she rolled her eyes.

"Daisy, you don't understand. Jamison has been out of the house for so long, that honestly, I'm used to it. Sad to say, but believe me that things are better when he was out the house. The entire atmosphere is much better," Amber explained.

"Wow! I knew things between you two weren't the best, but I didn't think it was this bad."

"I try not to stress you guys out with all my stupid relationship issues. Lately, I just been dealing with everything on my own."

"I hate when you do that Amber. We are best friends, I don't care what the issue is or what time you need to call. Bitch, call me and we will come up with ways to kill his ass and bury his body," Daisy fussed. She knew how sad and depressed Amber could get at times. It would break her heart knowing that something happened to her best friend and she couldn't do anything to change it.

"Oh, my god, you're nuts."

"So what, it's the truth though, and you know it is."

"Enough of my sob story though, where are we going tonight and what time?" Amber said, ready to change the subject.

"I wanted to go down Club Liv, but we can save that for Sunday. So, tonight, we going to a strip club and throw some racks. I want all of us to meet up around ten or eleven o'clock," Daisy explained.

"I'll be ready by then; I just need to get me a nap first."

"Damn, you such a grandma."

"I been at work since seven-thirty this morning. Bitch, I deserve to take a quick nap before turning up tonight."

"You know what, you have a point. You go ahead and take your nap. The last thing we need is for you to be in the strip club nodding off," Daisy said, causing the two of them to burst into laughter.

"Yea, because y'all asses like to post pictures of people at their worst."

"Girl, shut up, that was one damn time."

After laughing and enjoying the rest of their conversation, Amber exited her car and made her way inside of the house. As she got closer, she stopped to check the mail.

Once in the house with the door closed and locked behind

her, Amber took a seat on the sofa and got comfortable. She removed the flats from her feet and tucked them under her butt. She flipped through the mail, until a white envelope with her name caught her attention.

Tossing the additional mail in the end table, she looked over the odd envelope with a bit of concern. Not bothering to waste any more time, she ripped the mail open and was met with a great bit of surprise.

"Put your money where your mouth is, or shut the fuck up," a pissed off Latrell fussed, as he and Gunner stood in a nearby alley shooting dice with a few of their old friends.

"How the fuck you going to get mad because you out here losing all your money?" Gunner said as he laughed.

"Your ass not even playing, so shut up," Latrell continued to fuss as he turned his attention to Gunner.

"I'm not in no position to be giving you niggas my money in no damn dice game."

"How you know tonight wasn't going to be a lucky night for you?" one of their other friends said as he shook the dice in his hand.

Ring! Ring!

"It could have been, but we will never know," Gunner said as he pulled his phone out his pocket and answered it.

"Hello."

"Gunner..." Amber said through the tears.

"Yea Amber, what's going on? You good? Why you crying?" Gunner asked, immediately showing that he was concerned. As he waited for her to explain what was going on, he walked away from his friends.

"Are you busy? I need to speak with you and it's important," Amber questioned.

"A little, but what's going on?"

"Jamison and Lakesha..." Amber stated. Before Gunner would question what was going on with them, his phone started to beep with another incoming call. Taking the phone from his ear, he looked at the call and saw that it was his mother.

"Hold on, hold on, my mother calling on the other line," Gunner said to Amber before clicking over without giving her a time to object.

"Yea ma, what's going on?"

"Oh, my god, Gunner, please tell me you spoke to Kelsi!" Maria yelled into the phone in such a state of panic.

"She called me earlier asking about some money but nothing else," Gunner explained.

"She hasn't been answering her phone since she left out the house this morning. I have been calling back to back and I can't get ahold of her."

"Okay, I'm on my way," Gunner said without needing her to go in further detail. Immediately, he rushed over to where his friends were. Because he rode with Latrell, he couldn't just leave if he wanted to.

"Hello, Amber, you still there? What the hell is going on?" Gunner said as he clicked back over.

"Gunner, they are sleeping together," Amber finally admitted.

"What, who?" Gunner asked as he stopped mid-stride. He was stuck, hoping that she didn't say who he thought she was going to.

"Lakesha and Jamison."

1

––––––––

Frightened by the sound of Kimberly's tone when she called and told him Kelsi was missing, Jamison swerved through different lanes, rushing to get to his mother's house. As he fought to hold back his tears, he hoped for the best but he knew in heart that Kelsi wasn't okay. Honking his horn, he yelled at the cars in front of him to speed up.

"Move the fuck out the way!" he screamed.

It seemed like he couldn't get there fast enough. All he could think about was where Kelsi could be. He silently hoped that her sudden disappearance didn't have anything to do with the enemies he made in the streets over the last four years.

Fifteen minutes on the freeway seemed like hours. As he exited, he wanted someone to tell him that Kelsi was found as soon as he walked in the door. As he turned on to the side street, which was a shortcut to his mother's house, he pressed the gas harder, causing his speed to go up to eighty-five.

She has to be okay. Those motherfuckers know not to fuck with the Brown family, he thought, but his thoughts were interrupted by the ringing of his trap phone. Not wanting to answer it because he wasn't in the mood to be bothered, Jamison glanced at the caller ID and quickly decided against it.

"Hello," Jamison said as he answered and placed the phone to his ear.

"Hey, what's going on with you? I haven't talked to you all day," Lakesha said, showing her concern.

"My bad shorty, I been on some other shit all day."

"Is everything okay?"

"Shit was good until Kimberly called me saying that Kelsi was missing," Jamison explained to her.

"Wait, what?"

"Gunner didn't tell you?"

"I been ignoring him all day, so I haven't talked to him," Lakesha admitted

"Yea, well, haven't nobody talked to Kelsi since early this morning, and that's unlike her."

"You sure you guys aren't just jumping to conclusions? Y'all know how she can start doing something for a client and get side tracked."

"She was supposed to come get money from me earlier but never showed up. I didn't think nothing of it because I thought maybe she didn't need it anymore," Jamison explained.

"One thing Kelsi not doing is saying fuck money."

"Yea, well, I just pulled up to my mother house, so I'll hit you back."

"Family needs to be together during this difficult time. I'm in the area anyway, so I'll make my way to her house now."

"Bet," Jamison said before ending the call and quickly exiting his car.

Jamison rushed in the house where Kimberly sat on the couch. Upon entering the house, Jamison looked around, hoping he saw Kelsi somewhere hiding. Instead, he was only met with his two other sisters. Not seeing his mother, he walked over and took Kimberly in his arms for a tight hug. He then walked to Jessica, took a seat next to her, and wrapped his arms around her.

"How y'all feeling?" Jamison asked, trying to get a feel of where their heads were.

"Scared," Kimberly honestly answered.

"I just want her to come walking through that door and tell us she was out shopping like she always does," Jessica said as a single tear fell from her eyes.

"I know," Jamison said with a smirk on his face, agreeing with Jessica wishes before speaking again. "I put this shit on my life; I'm going to do everything in my power to get her back home safely and untouched."

"Whatever we have to do, we need to do it quickly because Kelsi is not made for that street shit," Jessica said after running her hands down her face.

Kelsi may have been the daughter of a street legend but, with the absence of Gunner, she had no one around to guide her on how to survive the Miami streets. Kimberly and Jessica were different; they had their father around to protect them but also teach them how to protect themselves.

"I love y'all man, I can't allow nothing to happen to y'all. I'm already fucked up about this shit as is. When the last time y'all talk or seen her?"

"Early in the day, but that's about it," Kimberly answered while her leg bounced uncontrollably.

"Around what time, because I called her around eleven and it rung until I got her voicemail?" Jessica asked, looking for clarification.

"I had to speak to her around ten-thirty and she was getting ready to get her day started," Kimberly answered.

"I spoke to her around eight in the morning and, from what I know, she spoke to Gunner before that. So, she been unaccounted for since eleven," Jamison acknowledged.

"Wow, that's too much time for us to not know her whereabouts."

"What happened to that app y'all had that track each other location?" Jamison asked as he tried to rack his brain on where Kelsi could be.

"She got pissed off at Jessica for fussing about where she was, so she turned her location off," Kimberly explained as she shook her head from side to side.

"What the fuck, she always doing dumb shit," Jamison spat out of frustration. Jessica gave him a stern look but, before she could tell Jamison about himself, Gunner had entered the house.

The scowl on Gunner's face didn't go unnoticed and the entire vibe in the room changed. For Gunner, it was as if no one else was in the room but him and Jamison. No matter how much his sisters attempted to talk to him, he wasn't trying to hear it. Due to the news that Amber had given him, his blood was boiling and fire was dancing in his eyes.

"You good bro?" Jamison asked while looking at Gunner as if there was a problem.

"I should ring your fucking neck, bitch!" Gunner roared as he rushed over to Jamison. Jamison jumped to his feet, preparing for a match, which caused Kimberly and Jessica to rush between them.

"What the fuck is the issue, this shit ain't my fault?" Jamison fussed.

Immediately, he began to think Gunner was blaming him for Kelsi going missing. People could say what they wanted about Jamison, but his sisters meant everything to him. He loved them and would do any and everything necessary for them.

"After everything I did for your stupid ass and this is how the fuck you betray me?" Gunner questioned, displaying his anger while balling up his fist. Gunner was so upset and had so much pent up aggression that he was ready to swing at any point.

"Gunner, please calm down!" Jessica screamed as she did her best to push Gunner away from Jamison. She continued to try and push the two apart but, unfortunately, Gunner wasn't moving a muscle.

"Nah, fuck that, this bitch ass nigga not about to keep playing in my face like he not fucking my bitch behind my back," Gunner continued to fuss.

"Man, fuck you. If you were dicking her down correctly, then she wouldn't be stuffing my dick down her throat," Jamison spat with a smirk on his face.

Hearing that caused Gunner to become angrier. So angry that he reached over his sisters and punched Jamison in the jaw. Jamison attempted to swing back but, due to Kimberly and Jessica standing between them, he ended up hitting Kimberly in the back of the head.

With so much going on, Gunner and Jamison began to fight. Kimberly and Jessica went from standing in the middle to now trying to break up their fight. Even though the efforts weren't successful, they tried their best. With all the yelling and commotion going on, Maria came rushing down the stairs to see what all was happening.

Maria was unpleased to see Gunner on top of Jamison, delivering blow after blow to his face. Truthfully, her heart was broken, and she was hurt by their actions. Here it was her youngest daughter was missing and her sons rather fight about other things instead of putting their brains together to figure out how to get her back.

"Gunner.... Jamison.... Gunner!" Maria screamed as she ran to where they were fighting. She immediately began to help the girls with breaking up the fight. Once they had Gunner off of a now bleeding Jamison, Maria roughly pushed Gunner until they were alone in the kitchen.

"What the fuck is your problem? Don't ever disrespect my house like that again with all that unnecessary ass fighting," Maria immediately fussed.

"He dead ass wrong for that shit ma," Gunner said in between breaths, trying to plead his case.

"What did he do that was so bad?" Maria asked. When she was in her bedroom, she couldn't understand what was being said, so she never knew the reason for the fight. What she did know was for Gunner to react based on emotions, his reasons must have been something serious.

"He slept with Lakesha," Gunner revealed to her.

Maria took a deep breath and took a moment to think before she spoke. On one hand, she understood why Gunner was upset and why he reacted the way he did. However, on the other hand, she couldn't deal with this right now. Maria may have liked Lakesha and dealt with her when she needed to, but she wasn't worth the headache in her opinion.

"I understand that you mad, I really do, but is she more important than what we are going through now?" Maria questioned.

"You right ma, I'm tripping. I lost sight of what was more important."

"You deal with that shit accordingly after we get situated here. But, remember, she is just as guilty as Jamison is. So, don't get mad at one and not the other."

"I know ma, I know," Gunner said with a hint of sadness in his voice. Regardless of anything, he loved Lakesha and, at one point, he had thoughts of marrying her. But, with this coming out and with Jamison basically admitting that they fooled around, he knew he would never be able to forgive either of them.

"So, where are we with the Kelsi situation?" Gunner asked, changing the topic.

"I reached out to your father's old detective friend, Keith, and he should be on his way to speak with us. Typically, she would have to be missing for twenty-four hours before MPD can do anything, but he is willing to help," Maria informed.

"Ma, you sure this don't have anything going on with the business?"

"I asked Jamison if he had any enemies and he keep telling me no. All I have is his word to go off of, that's it."

I hope he wouldn't lie about anything as important as this."

"Yea, I hope not either," Maria said as their minds began to wonder.

2

Jamison parked his car and hopped out with a mean mug on his face. He had just made it to the trap. He couldn't go home because his mind was all messed up. He needed a place where he could think of a plan to get his sister back. Going home would mean that he would have to face Amber. He didn't know how much she knew about him and Lakesha and he wasn't trying to find out.

As he walked up to the entrance, he thought about the fucked-up way Gunner tried to fight him like they were still little kids. A part of him wanted to take a ride back to Maria's house and wait for Gunner to come outside, so he could beat his ass. He never wanted his mother and sister to see the two of them fight. The more he thought about the disrespect, the angrier he became.

"Damn!" Jamison yelled as he stared at Dave and Sham, who were already at the trap.

"What the fuck happened to you?" Dave asked him, putting his phone down on the desk in front of him. "You're over there sweating like a motherfucker.

Jamison fought to catch his breath before he spoke. "My

sister is missing. We don't know what happened to her, but we know it ain't cool."

"What sister?" Sham asked.

"What you mean missing?" Dave added.

"I mean gone. She ain't been answering the phone. It's unlike Kelsi to disappear like this."

"Damn!" Sham said as he sat down on the chair that was on the side of him.

"Fuck, they're getting down like that?" Dave said. There was nothing else he could say. He stood up from behind the desk and walked over to Jamison, who had tears in his eyes. "It's gone be alright man."

"We gone get her back," Sham assured him, not being sure of where to start looking. All he knew was that he wasn't going to stop trying to find Kelsi.

Jamison wiped his crying eyes with the back of his hand before he made eye contact with Sham. "To make matters worse. Me and that nigga Gunner just got into it at my mom's house over that bitch Lakesha. I guess someone told him we were fucking around, so the nigga tried to check me. That motherfucka always trying to play the big man."

"Y'all don't need to be at each other's neck at a sensitive time like this. I don't see why that shit even came up in conversation. The focus should be getting Kelsi back."

"I know, Sham, but the nigga came to me with the shit. What was I supposed to do, let him punk me?"

"No, you were supposed to tell him what I'm telling you. Focus on your little sister. Y'all personal shit can wait."

"I feel you. I'm just sick and tired of Gunner acting like I don't mean shit. He acted like he can say and do anything to me because I'm younger than him, but I run these streets. He lost that right when he went to prison."

Sham shook his head in disbelief. "O, you mean when he did four years for you?"

Jamison looked at Sham as he came back to reality. "I don't want to talk about this shit no more," he said as he looked over at Dave. "Have you heard anything on the streets about someone taking a young girl?"

"Nawl, no one is talking about anything," Dave answered. "If you want, I could…"

Their conversation was interrupted by the sound of Jamison's notifications going off. "Hold on, who the fuck is this?" As he read the text message that came to his phone, his hands began to shake. With lowered eyes, he couldn't hold back the anger that burned inside of him. It was time to contact everyone who had ever owed him a favor.

"What's going on?" Dave asked.

"Sham, can we have the room?" Jamison asked.

"It's all good. I'm about to get in the streets. Maybe I can find out if someone knows anything. I'll hit you in a few hours."

"Alright," Jamison answered as the two of them bumped fists.

Dave knew something was up with Jamison by the way he was acting. "What's going on; who was that- that text you?"

"These motherfuckers are playing dirty as fuck. They want me to give them a hundred thousand dollars for them to spare Kelsi life."

"They must be out of their fucking mind. How soon are they talking?"

"They didn't say. All they said was that they know I got some money put up somewhere and I bet not play no games with them."

"Damn."

"I got to figure this shit out."

"You need to call Gunner. The two of y'all can make something happen. I know you are mad at him, but you need him right now."

Jamison became enraged as he picked up one of the chairs

and threw it at the wall, breaking it to pieces. "I don't need that motherfucker for shit. Fuck him and his bitch. All I need to do is put something together. Fuck Gunner."

"I didn't mean it like that. I was just trying to help."

"Don't try to help by telling me I need that nigga because I don't. I haven't needed him for shit in the last four years. I know how to handle this shit. Gunner don't know nothing about the streets."

"Look, I'm gone go and check on a few things. I'll be back later when you cool off. It seems like any mention of Gunner name got you hot."

Jamison stared in the opposite direction of Dave. He didn't want to hear nothing else he had to say. His heart was hurting because he didn't have the money to save his baby sister. Not only that, he had too much pride to tell anyone that it could be his fault that his sister was taken in the first place. He had reached an all-time low. His greed and thirst for power had affected his entire family.

With Dave and Sham being gone, he began to reflect on what was going on. Looking up, he cried like he cried the day his father died. The empty in his heart had been buried for years. Kelsi, he called out. I never meant to suck you up into this street shit. I promise I'm going to find you and bring you back home safe.

GUNNER SAT in the living room at his mother's house. He couldn't go home and face Lakesha because his anger and disappointment would be all bad for her. He wasn't the kind of man to put his hands on a woman, but he wanted to slap the fuck out of her for making him look stupid.

He trusted her with everything he had. He could have forgiven her if she had dipped here and there with anyone else, but his brother and his friends were off limits. He would never try to fool around with anyone she knew. He respected her enough not to hurt her to that extent. She hurt him so badly that he didn't want to look at any other woman for a long time.

"Are you okay, baby?" Maria asked as she rubbed his shoulder.

"I'm good, Ma; I'm just worried about Kelsi. I know she gone be okay."

"Yeah, I'm worried too, but we have to keep praying, That's all we can do at this point. We have to pray that God is going to keep her safe, no matter where she is or who she is with."

Kimberly walked in on the conversation wearing her pajamas. She had gotten dressed earlier that morning, but hearing about Kelsi caused her to stay at home. She'd been trying to keep busy all day to keep from being stressed out, but nothing was working. She had never been in a situation where she couldn't get ahold of her baby sister and it was driving her crazy.

"No disrespect, ma, but God is the reason she is missing; why would we pray to him? He could have protected her but, instead, he let people take her," she cried. "Why would God let something happen to Kelsi?"

"No-no. Don't you go questioning God. I need you to get a hold of yourself, Kimberly. Kelsi would want you to be strong."

Gunner got up out his seat and held Kimberly, as she buried her head in his chest. He was weak himself, but he knew he had to stay strong for the rest of the family. All he could do was assure them that they were not alone. He rubbed Kimberly's hair as he watched his mother break down and cry.

"It's gone be okay. Y'all got to be strong. Right now is not the time to break down. Whoever she with gone make a wrong move. Trust me when I tell you this. They not stupid enough to hurt her because they don't want to start a war. Miami ain't ready for what would happen if something happens to Kelsi."

Kimberly broke away from Gunner. "You're right. I'm going to go back into her room and see if I can find anything. I've been looking for something all day, but I don't know what I'm looking for."

"What about her schedule? If we find out the last event she did, we can go there and ask questions."

"She never told me about her clients," Kimberly responded. "Wait, maybe she posted something on her social media. Sometimes, her location is on there."

Gunner looked down at his phone. "Sham calling me. Let me take this."

He walked into the back room and answered the phone. After talking on the phone, he made his way back into the living room and headed towards the front door. Seeing that he was in a rush, Maria stopped him before he could open it.

"What's going on?" she asked, hoping he found Kelsi.

"Sham is outside. He says he have to tell me something important. I don't want to talk business in here because it's some things that you shouldn't hear. I'm not trying to stress you out." He smiled.

Maria smiled back at him. "Be safe son. And please don't leave without telling me. The last thing I need is for you to come up missing too."

"I'm not going nowhere, ma. I don't want to leave you alone. I'll be right back."

Gunner made his way outside. As he walked to Sham's car, he noticed that Lakesha was calling him. He couldn't deal with her, so he pressed ignore. She called right back, so he ignored her call again and placed her on his blocked list. He didn't want to hear her disgusting voice. There was a time that her voice was the sexiest thing he'd ever heard. But, he couldn't stand her and everything about her made him sick to his stomach.

"What's going on Sham?" he greeted as he got in the passenger seat.

"I heard what happened to Kelsi. My bad for not answering your calls earlier. You know if I had known she was missing, I would have been answered. Shit, I would have called you first."

"It's all good. I know you been doing some heavy shit in the streets. It's all love," Gunner said as he adjusted himself in his seat. "What did you have to tell me?"

Sham took a deep breath to prepare himself for what he was about to say. He knew that saying this would change him and Jamison's friendship forever, but that wasn't important. "I was at the trap today with Jamison and Dave. Jamison received a text message that caused him to instantly break out in sweats. I mean, ya boy was shaking and all the shit."

"Is that right. Who text him?" Gunner asked.

"He never said who it was. He did ask me to leave the room. I said okay, but I knew something was up by the way he was shaking so bad that he could barely hold his phone, so I listened from the other room for a few minutes before I left." Sham held his head down. It hurt him to tell Gunner what happened next, but he had to.

"Keep going. You got to tell me what happened."

"I'm going to tell you, but I don't want you to react ignorant."

"You better fucking tell me right now, Sham."

"He said that someone text him and told him they had Kelsi."

Gunner screamed. "What? He knows who got Kelsi and he ain't called me. I'm gone kill that mother fucker when I get my hands on him."

Sham put his hand up. "Hold on, Gunner. There's more."

Gunner pinched his lips. "What?" he said through pushed air.

"Whoever got Kelsi wants a hundred thousand dollars in return for her life."

"So, what he saying he going to do?" Gunner asked out of concern.

"Man, I don't know, but I do know that he doesn't have that type of money. When I left the trap, he was wildin'," Sham informed.

"Man, do he know who it is or whom the text came from?"

"Nah... but he is out here making a lot of enemies out in these streets."

"Like who? Who the most recent? Matter fact, Sham, you know the game; who standing out in your mind?" Gunner questioned as he pulled on his beard.

"Cornell," Sham blurted out.

"Cornell, from back in the day. The one we use to kick it with?"

"Yea... him and Jamison was supposed to team up and take over the entire Dade Count-" Sham started saying before he was cut off by Gunner.

"Team up? Is this nigga fucking serious? We worked too damn hard to team up with anyone," Gunner spat, showing just how upset he truly was.

"Honestly, I don't know. However, I do know that he burnt his ass. Ran up in his house and took all his work," Sham informed.

"So, this shit is personal, but what the fuck Kelsi has to do with anything?" Gunner asked out of frustration.

"I wasn't there, but from what I heard was Cornell mother was there and got caught in the cross fire."

Gunner took a deep breath and ran his hands down his face. After a few seconds of silence, Gunner finally spoke up. "Let me get out of here and clear my mind. I'll hit your line later, but thanks for that information. Do me a favor though, keep your ears to the streets."

"Will do," Sham said, as Gunner began to get out the car.

"Aye Gunner, do me a favor and protect your brother. I did

all I could do for him and y'all family, but he too far gone to listen to anyone on the outside."

"I hear you, Sham, but I can't help someone that doesn't want to be helped," Gunner said before he closed the door and walked away.

3

———

Gunner walked into his mother's house with a number of emotions running through him. He was mad, sad, pissed off, and very much frustrated. A part of himself was beating himself up because he felt like he was wrong for coming in and acting off emotions. However, at the same time, if Jamison had information on the whereabouts of Kelsi, then the first person he should have come to was his family.

"Is everything okay?" Maria asked as she stopped from wiping off the counter and turned her attention to her son.

"Yea, mommy, I just have a lot on my mind, that's all," Gunner answered. He walked over to the fridge and grabbed a water. As he removed the top and began to quench his thirst, he listened to what his mother had to say.

"Your phone was sitting over there ringing. I glanced at it thinking that it was someone important, but it was someone stored under Toni."

"Did you answer?" Gunner asked as he walked over to where his phone was sitting.

"No, was I supposed to?"

"I meannnn...." Gunner started saying, as he allowed his words to drag while he read the text she had sent.

Toni: Hey, give me a call as soon as possible. It's important!

"Who is Toni?" Maria asked, pulling his attention from what he was reading.

"Someone I work with," Gunner said. He didn't need to elaborate because his mother was smart enough to understand what that meant and to not ask any additional questions.

"What was Sham taking about?" Maria questioned, internally praying that they found some type of answers.

"He heard about the situation and wanted to see what he can do to help," Gunner lied. He didn't want to tell his mother that someone was holding her for ransom, and that neither him or Jamison had the money to get her back. It would break Maria's heart, and she didn't need any additional stress on her.

"Sham has always been good to us and our family. Whenever the girls and I would see him out, he made sure to make sure we were okay," Maria said with a pleased smile on her face.

Knowing that even though Sham felt like Jamison was going off the deep end, he still remained loyal to his family. That alone caused Gunner to respect him much more. They always been boys but, when Gunner got locked up, they lost contact. Gunner may have felt some type of way then, but now that all had changed.

"Yea, anyone that could stand by Jamison side through all of this must be a good guy," Gunner said, causing his mother to giggle to herself.

"Yea, well, I just hope you and Jamison can work out everything that's going on. Lord knows I hate when all of y'all get to arguing and carrying on."

"I know ma, but that's not what you need to stress about. Whatever happens happen, but either way he family and, in tough times, we going to be there for one another. However, I need to go make a phone call, so give me a minute," Gunner said before placing a reassuring kiss on her forehead and walking down the basement.

Once he was alone by himself, he took a seat on the sofa and placed a call back to Toni and waited for her to answer the phone. After about three rings, she finally answered the phone.

"What's up, you called me?" Gunner asked, jumping right into the reason of the call.

"Yea, I called you about what we spoke about earlier."

"Yea, what about it?"

"I can't come that way tonight or tomorrow. So, I need you to come by here," Toni explained.

"You can't send someone my way?" Gunner asked. He didn't want to leave his family alone and, at the same time, he really didn't want to take that long ride to Toni's house.

"Unfortunately, no, I'm having a family emergency."

After taking a deep breath, Gunner thought a little harder on the situation. Even though he didn't want to take that drive, he sucked it up and decided to do it. As a leader of his own and someone starting his own empire, he had to sacrifice and get the things he didn't want to do... done. Plus, he needed the money more than anything, due to the situation Jamison had gotten them in.

"Okay, I'm on my way then. I'm having a family situation of my own, so give me a few minutes and I'll be there shortly," Gunner let her know.

"No problem, everything ready for whenever you can get here. No rush, just text me when you about five to ten minutes away."

"Bet!" Gunner said as he stood up from the sofa.

"Thank you, Gunner," Toni said in a soft voice.

"No problem, see you in a few," Gunner said before he ended the call.

WITHIN AN HOUR AND A HALF, Gunner was pulling up to Toni's house. Although he didn't want to take the drive, he took the time to sit back and reflect on what was going on in his life.

The thought of confronting Lakesha about the things she had done with Jamison crossed his mind and, the more he thought of it, the angrier he became. He couldn't run from the problems they were having and, truthfully, he knew he wouldn't be able to forgive her either.

Gunner was a grown man, a man that wasn't going to sit and play games with any female. He learned a long time ago that bitches came and go and, because of the business he was in, many females tried to stick around and be a ride-or-die, when they only wanted one thing... the money. Gunner's main goal was to get back to where he used to be, and now he had to think hard on if Lakesha was helping or hurting him in the process.

As Gunner pulled up in the garage, he noticed that Toni was opening the side door. She was wearing a pair of black biker shorts that came down to her knees, an oversized t-shirt, with pink UGG slippers on her feet. Although she was clearly in her pajamas, her beauty couldn't go unnoticed. Gunner shook his head from side to side, trying to get all the sexual thoughts out of his mind. He couldn't deny the fact that he was attracted to her, but it wasn't the right time to act on those thoughts.

"Leave the doors unlocked and come inside. My peoples with handle everything out here," Toni ordered, as soon as Gunner opened the driver's side door.

He did what he was told and followed Toni in her house. Toni led Gunner to the kitchen where she was cleaning up the food she had just cooked. It was against her norm to have anyone she was doing business with in her personal space, but things with Gunner were different.

Toni may not have known Gunner that well, but the way she felt when she was around him was something she couldn't explain. He made her feel like she was safe in his presence, and that was the one thing she like the most. She may had played hard to get, but that was just her protecting her heart. She had been hurt before and she never wanted to feel that type of pain again.

"You want something to eat?" Toni asked, breaking the silence between the two of them. Gunner was deep into his phone, so he wasn't paying her any attention until she spoke up.

"I'm good, I ate before I came," Gunner lied. He wasn't hungry at all. With everything he had going on, the last thing he wanted to do was eat anything.

"Okay, well, it shouldn't take them long. Like I said, everything was placed to the side and ready," Toni said.

"At this point, I'm not really in no rush. You good though? I know you said something was going on."

"Yea... I'm good. I just have a lot on my mind, that's all."

"Oh-" Gunner started to say before he was cut off by the sound of small feet hitting the hardwood floors.

"Momma Toni, guess what," Mario said in excitement as he came running into the kitchen. He stopped in mid-run when he saw that Gunner and Toni's eyes was trained on him.

"Yes, Mario, what's going on?"

"Hey, I know you," Mario said, not answering Toni and forgetting what he had come downstairs for.

"What's up lil man?" Gunner greeted.

"Mario!" Toni called out, getting his attention. Mario was young and naive, he would make friends with anyone he came across. Because Toni knew this, she did everything she could to protect him from everyone. She didn't believe Gunner would do anything to harm him, but it was just the precautions that she took no matter what.

"Oh, yea, I'm sorry. Guess what though?"

"What?" Toni said, ready for him to get to the point.

"I got a lot of kills in COD," Mario announced in excitement, causing Gunner to laugh to himself.

"Mario, I told you about playing that game. I don't want you playing that mess; it's too much and you are way too young," Toni fussed.

"But, but it's fun," he tried to protest.

"But nothing, now let's go. I'm turning it off and breaking the game. Who even bought you that crap anyway?" Toni fussed as she grabbed his hand.

"My mama," Mario answered, snitching on Toni's mother.

Gunner remained seated at the breakfast bar and shook his head from side to side while laughing to himself. A few minutes later, Toni came walking back to the kitchen with the Call of Duty game in her hand. Tossing it on the counter, she rolled her eyes and took a deep breath.

"If you have Xbox or knows someone that do, you can have that dumb game," Toni said.

"I don't play games baby girl; you better off trashing that," Gunner responded.

"Oh okay," Toni said before tucking her lips and raising her eye brows.

"I didn't know you had a child though."

"I don't!" Toni spat.

"Oh... not too be all up in your business, but I asked because he called you momma," Gunner pointed out.

"He's my nephew, but I take care of him more than his mother does. It's hard to explain, really," Toni said, not wanting to go deeper into the conversation. Gunner nodded his head, indicating that he understood what she was saying.

"Everything good with your situation though?" Toni asked.

"Honestly, no."

"What's going on?"

Gunner took a deep breath before he spoke. He really didn't want to talk about it anymore because he was internally beating himself up with the situation. However, he felt like he could vent to Toni without being judged.

"I have so much shit going on right now. For starters, my youngest sister came up missing."

"Oh, my god, what?" Toni interrupted with concern.

"Yea, no one has talked to her since about noon this morning. Then, to make matters worse, I found out some shit about my brother which made me want to beat the shit out of him," Gunner went on to say.

"I'm not sure what you two are mad at each other about, but I'm sure your sister's whereabouts are more important than any of that mess."

"You right it is but, at the time, I was so pissed, I just fucked him up," Gunner admitted, while showing how disappointed he was of himself.

"You should never allow someone to get you that upset to the point where you lose sight of what's more important."

"Yea, well, I know that now."

"So, what are y'all doing about your sister?" Toni asked out of concern.

"I found out through someone else that my brother received a ransom text. Come to find out, he fucked someone over and hurt their family and, in return, this what they decided to do. This not my battle to fight but, when you start bringing innocent people in it, that's when my hands are tied and I have to run to the fucking rescue," Gunner explained.

"So, what's the issue with the ransom?"

"The amount. I'm just getting my feet back in the game; I'm not in no position to pull a hundred thousand dollars out my ass. Jamison got himself in this shit and, sadly, his stupid ass doesn't even have that type of money."

"I thought he was running the streets since you had gotten locked up?" Toni asked with a confused look on her face, causing Gunner to snicker. Yea, a hundred thousand dollars seemed like a lot of money but, when you been hustling the streets and your name ring bells in the streets, that's play money to you. Toni just couldn't understand why his brother was claiming to not have it.

"That man is living in a fantasy world. He thinks he really out here running the streets and doing his thing but, in all actuality, he is doing more damage than anything. He running his mouth more than he is running them fucking streets. That alone explains how it's so easy for me to come home from a four-year bid and jump back in the game so quick."

"Wow!"

"At this point, I just have to make some things shake and get my sister home and safe. I'm going to stress myself out until I do so," Gunner vented.

"Can I ask you a question?"

"What?"

"You break your neck for everyone else, who's there for you when you need it?" Toni questioned.

"No one," Gunner admitted.

"That's the issue. Eventually Gunner, you must allow people to face the consequences of their own actions. This may not be a good situation for that, but you're allowing people to use you as a doormat. You seem like too much of a good guy for that," Toni preached, causing Gunner to think hard about the words she was saying.

"I don't mean to lecture you, and I apologize if I'm over stepping my boundaries. It's just I'm going through the same shit with my sister, so I know how it feels to be in your position," Toni added.

"You good, I understand what you saying. I was just always raised that family comes first. So, no matter the shit my brother does, I always run to clean up the mess he makes."

"And that's probably why he continues to make up the mess. People learn from their mistakes, but you can't learn anything if you don't understand that you made a mistake in the first place."

"You're absolutely correct."

"Right, well, anyway. I can give you the money to bring your sister home."

"I can't take that from you Toni," Gunner said as he shook his head from side to side.

"Put your pride to the side and accept the money. I'm not expecting you to pay the money back or anything like that. I'm simply helping you out because I know how it feel to be in that type of situation, to feel helpless and having your hands tied," Toni explained.

She may not have been in the exact situation that Gunner was in, but the situation with her father was somewhat similar. He was taking away from her and, unlike Gunner, there was nothing Toni could do until the judge said he could be released.

"I'll make sure you get your money back."

"If that makes you happy, then okay," Toni said, ending the conversation there. Gunner and Toni remained in the kitchen for a few extra minutes before Gunner left to return home.

4

~3 DAYS LATER~

"So, where are we going?" Kelsi asked as she sat in the back of a minivan. Her hands where cuffed behind her back, and there were cuffs on her ankles as well. Although she was scared, she did nothing to show it. She didn't want to show any sides of weakness, so they could play on that. Also, she did want to do anything stupid, causing them to have to harm her in any way.

"Why is there not tape across her mouth?" the driver asked, showing that he was growing annoyed with her.

"Because your stupid ass didn't stop and get any," the guy to the right of her fussed.

"Ronny, fuck you!" the driver spat while slipping up and revealing a name.

As both of the young guys fussed back and forth, Kelsi sat with her lips tucked and her eyes shifting from one guy to the next. She could tell that they were some bottom guys and wasn't experienced at all with kidnapping anyone. They were dropping names left and right, didn't have any of the needed supplies and, to make matters worse, only one of them kept their face mask on.

"Aye, all y'all shut the fuck up. You niggas act like y'all fucking stupid or something. Sit back, enjoy the ride, and shut the fuck up!" the masked man yelled after pulling his mask up over his mouth.

"If I need to shut up, then just say it," Kelsi said as she looked around at all the guys.

"Sweetheart, do me a favor and keep it mute for the rest of the ride. Once we get to where we going and we turn you over to the people we need to, you can all one hundred questions that you wish to ask," he said to her in a calm tone.

"No problem," Kelsi said as she smiled at him and turned her attention out of the window.

She had no clue where she was going or what was in store for her. However, what she did know was that she was ready to go home. Every moment that she had alone since she was kidnapped, she said a silent prayer that her family would find her before it was too late. She had no clue what had got her in the situation or what needed to be done to get her out. But, she had faith that her brother was smart enough to get her out.

Before the four guys she was with now had come to get her, she was locked in some type of apartment bedroom. The door to the room remained locked at all times and there were bars on the window, so she had no way to escape. She was only left with a bed, a TV, a case of water, and three meals were brought to her throughout the day.

Within twenty minutes, they were parking in front of what looked like an office building. Before exiting the van, the three guys whom revealed their face, placed the masks over their face. Kelsi shook her head from side to side, not understanding any of their logic.

They pulled her out of the van and led her into the main entrance of the building. As they walked down the empty hall, confusion came over Kelsi. She refused to believe that Cornell, whom was walking in her direction, had anything to do with this.

"Cornell?" Kelsi called out as she stopped walking.

"Don't cause a scene in this hallway, just keep walking," Cornell said as she shook his head in disappointment.

He wasn't disappointed in her; he was disappointed in the guys he sent to be responsible for her. He gave them specific directions; one being to make sure that her face was covered the entire time, but here she was with nothing. If everything went as smoothly as planned, he made a mental note to handle their stupid asses.

Two of the guys continued to walk down the hall, until they reached a door that led to an empty room. As Kelsi looked around, she saw that the room was empty, yet clean. It was nothing like the place she held before, and she prayed they didn't keep her here long.

Once the guys exited the room, leaving Kelsi alone, she immediately rushed to the closed door in hope to hear what was being said.

"Y'all niggas do whatever it is that y'all want, huh?" Kelsi could hear Cornell asking with annoyance in his voice.

"You said bring her here in one piece, and that's what we did."

"No, dick head, he talking about covering her eyes and mouth. I told y'all about that, but y'all so smart, y'all dumb."

"Tay, your ass wasn't saying shit then, so shut your ass up now."

"Yea, okay, don't get fucked up in here."

"Both of y'all shut up. Go get in position because his ass should be here in any minute now."

"So, what you going to do with her?" one of the guys questioned.

"Depends, if they play shit cool, then the results won't be

too drastic. But, one wrong move from Jamison and I want her head served on a silver platter," Cornell answered.

Those words alone caused Kelsi to back away from the door with fear. She was scared because she knew Cornell enough to know he meant business. If Gunner was coming to rescue her, she would feel better because she would put his pride aside to do what was needed. However, Jamison was different; his pride and ego was too big to just do what was asked of him.

Moments later, the door to the room opened and Cornell walked inside. He closed the door behind him and hit the light switch. As the lights came on, the two of them came face to face.

This was a man that attended her father's funeral. A man whom her brothers trusted and treated as family. A man whom looked out for her whenever she was in his hood. She just couldn't understand why someone she trusted could do this to her and her family.

"Why?" Kelsi asked while looking Cornell directly in the eyes.

"It's business, never personal shorty," Cornell said as he shrugged his shoulder. He removed a set of keys out his back pocket.

"Turn around, so I can uncuff you. Make one wrong move and I swear shit will get ugly in here," Cornell warned, causing Kelsi to slowly turn around.

With her back and cuffed hands facing Cornell, he uncuffed her legs and wrist. As soon as the cuffs were removed, she quickly turned around to come face to face with him. She now didn't trust him as far as she could throw him. The last thing she wanted to do was give him a chance to harm her.

"Karma is a powerful thing," Kelsi spat before Cornell left out the room with a sneaky grin plastered on his face.

～

"WHERE THE FUCK have you been for the last three days Gunner?" Lakesha screamed, as she stood at the top of the steps with her hands on her hip.

Instead of answering her, Gunner pushed past her and continued to the bedroom. He was on a mission to come in, get a few things, and go on about his business. The last thing he was about to do was argue and bullshit with or anyone else.

"You so fucking disrespectful. You don't come home for three days; then, you want to waltz your ass up in here and act like shit all sweet," Lakesha continued to argue as she followed behind Gunner.

"Man, get the fuck out my face with that bullshit you spitting."

"Bullshit? Oh, it's bullshit when you do it but, when I don't come home, it's a damn problem."

"You can do as you please, like the fuck you been doing," Gunner spat over his shoulder.

He wasn't trying to feed into her bullshit. However, he knew that eventually he would have to deal with her and the problems they faced. Only issue was that, at this point, he was done with the relationship. The time he spent away from her, he used the time to reflect. As much as Gunner hated to admit it, he knew she meant no good to him and he had to do what was best for him.

"What the fuck is that supposed to mean?"

"Exactly what the fuck I said."

"If it's something on your mind, then say that shit," Lakesha snapped as she stood in the middle of their bedroom. Gunner, who was now sitting on the end of the bed, took a deep breath and looked Lakesha directly in the eyes.

"Why you doing this, huh? You know you fucked up. So, let's not sit in here and pretend like I'm some fucking fool."

"I don't know what the fuck you talking about," Lakesha lied. She was well aware that he knew about the affair she had with Jamison. However, she wasn't going to admit to it until she was no longer able to deny the affair.

"Oh, so you weren't fucking Jamison?" Gunner asked. Before a lie could roll off of Lakesha's tongue, Gunner continued to speak. "Before you lie, just know that I have some pictures of you and this nigga tonguing each other down."

"It wasn't even like that, I swear," Lakesha pleaded. Knowing now that she wasn't able to lie anymore, she used the tactic that usual got her out of most situations... crying. Tears immediately filled her eyes and began to stain her face. Only difference was this time, those tears did nothing to move Gunner.

"Then, how was it? You let me know, since clearly I don't know shit."

"Yes, we kissed, but it was one time and one time-" Lakesha started saying but was cut off by Gunner laughing.

"I see clearly you and him didn't sit and get the story straight. You making matters worse for yourself now. He already put me up on game that the two of y'all been fucking with each other. You lying about it is not going to do anything but piss me off even more."

"I just don't know what else you want me to say."

"Nothing, what's done is done and there is nothing you or him can do to change it. Hell, even if it was, I'm sure you two selfish mother fuckers wouldn't do anything about it anyway."

"Yes, I would."

"Okay, tell me anything," Gunner said as he stood up from the bed and walked over to the dresser that stored his clothes.

"So, what now?"

"You go your separate ways and I'll go mine."

"So, I fuck up once and now you calling it quits between us? After I have held you down and been there for you while you did a four-year bid."

"You call coming to see me one a month, whenever the fuck

you feel like it, holding me down. Or better yet, having me arguing with you to put my money, the money I was out here hustling for, on my books. If that's what the fuck you call holding me down, then you could have kept that shit."

"You know what Gunner, fuck you! You want to go out and live your life, then that's fine with me. However, don't fucking come running back to me when you realize that no other bitch is going to love you like I do."

"As long as you don't call me when you realize that Jamison won't leave his wife for you," Gunner snapped as he shrugged his shoulders.

Deciding to not respond to what Gunner had said to her, Lakesha rolled her eyes and left out the room. Walking to the kitchen, she poured herself a glass of Vodka straight.

After throwing the drink back, she leaned up against the island and began to rack her brain on the matter. She was so upset and pissed off. Yea, she was made at Jamison for running his mouth but, at the same time, she was mad at herself.

She couldn't believe that she allowed the affair to get that far and for Gunner finding out about it. She loved Gunner, but she yearned for the attention while he was gone. No matter her reason for any of it, she knew she had no business allowing it to get to this point.

Although she was pissed with herself, she couldn't shake the feeling that the female she spotted with Gunner may have added to his reasons for leaving her alone. She was to blame, true indeed, but she would be crushed to know she was losing her man to another woman. Just the thought of him living his best life with some female took her from being hurt to pissed.

Thinking about Gunner loving another woman, fucking another woman and, better yet, giving another woman every-thing he was supposed to give her caused Lakesha to become so upset that she threw the glass she was holding against the wall.

Lakesha remained in the kitchen taking shots of the Vodka,

while allowing her mind to run rapidly. When Gunner walked down the steps and into the entry of the kitchen, Lakesha didn't bother to try and hide the tears that were rolling down her face, and Gunner didn't bother to acknowledge them.

"I'll be back later this week to get the rest of my things," Gunner announced as he held a duffle bag in his hand. Without waiting for a response, Gunner threw the bag over his shoulder and left out the house, leaving her where she was.

5

~ FOUR HOURS LATER ~

"Tavon said all you have to do is send the text and Cornell should get it," Latrell said as he sat in the driver's seat of the car.

"He will get it from Jamison number though, right?" Gunner questioned.

"Yea, that's what he saying. Before we split up, he said that he already set it up."

"This damn technology, man." Gunner said as he shook his head before pressing send on the app.

After texting Cornell from his personal phone and not hearing back from him, Gunner felt that he had to do something different. He knew that Jamison wasn't going to be cooperative and help him get their sister back, so he didn't bother trying with him. After linking up with Latrell and his brother, he came up with a way to get shit done.

Tavon informed them about a texting app that allows you to send text messages from a different number. They had everything set up already, for when and where they would meet.

However, Cornell would be in a rude awakening when they came face to face.

. . .

305-999-1234: Okay! Step out the car with the bag and walk over to the door.

GUNNER READ the text and informed Latrell what the plan was. The two of them stepped out the car, and Gunner walked over to the trunk to remove the duffle bags that held the money. Once they had everything in hand, the two of them began walking towards the door. Just as they were approaching the door, three buff guys wearing security t-shirts came walking out the door.

"Drop the bags off to the side, step back, and hold out your arms," one of them demanded.

Gunner and Latrell did as they were told. They allowed the guys to do their job and check them. This wasn't Gunner or Latrell's first rodeo with this, and Gunner knew Cornell well enough to know what not to bring with them. They didn't have any weapons on them, but they did have other means of protection.

After being pat down, the men checked the duffle bags, making sure that only money was inside. Pleased with everything, one of the guys disappeared back into the building.

Moments later, he returned, followed by Cornell and some other guy. The three guys picked up the duffle bags and all disappeared back in the building, leaving them alone.

"Look what we have here," Cornell said as he laughed to himself. Coming face to face with Gunner and Latrell, he wasn't sure what to expect really.

Cornell had no plans on hurting Kelsi; in all actuality, he just wanted everything that he felt belonged to him. He didn't bring Gunner into the issue because it wasn't Gunner's battle to fight. Jamison was the one that caused the problem, so Cornell felt as if Jamison needed to deal with it.

"Sup!" Gunner said in return. He wasn't in the mood for any of the extra conversation. He came in here with one agenda and one agenda only.

"Truthfully, I'm actually surprised to see you here G," Cornell admitted, while calling Gunner by his childhood street nickname.

"I'm not sure why you so surprised, you do have my sister with you. What you thought I was going to do, let her stay with you?" Gunner said with sarcasm.

"No, but I would have expected for Jamison to man up and deal with the consequences of his actions."

"Well, I'm here now, so..." Gunner said, growing slightly annoyed.

Everyone who was familiar with the relationship Gunner and Jamison had with one another knew that Gunner always ran to his rescue. Yea, Gunner led Cornell to believe that he was meeting with Jamison but, even so, he was a fool to believe he would be meeting him alone.

"Cornell, your problems with Jamison is just that- your problems with Jamison. We not even here for any of that bull-shit," Latrell said, finally speaking out.

Being that he knew both guys very well, Latrell knew how tense this situation could get.

Gunner didn't play when it came to his family or anyone he loved, and Cornell was the same way. Plus, Latrell had a minor dislike for the way that Gunner handled things in regards to Jamison. Especially, knowing all the disrespect he got in return.

"You wanted a particular amount of money, and I brought that with me. All I ask is that you don't lay a fucking finger on my sister and hand her over to me."

"How you get the money?" Cornell asked with squinted eyes. Remembering what Dave told to him about Gunner possibly getting back into the game, he felt this money was a good one to question him about it.

"Does it matter? Just know that it's all there."

"I'll be the judge of that," Cornell snapped.

After another ten minutes, one of the guys returned to where they were and informed Cornell that all the money was counted and good. In return, Cornell gave him the okay to get Kelsi and bring her out. Within seconds, they were pulling Kelsi out to them.

"It's always nice doing business with the Brown's family," Cornell sarcastically said while Kelsi was aggressively pushed in Gunner's direction. Before he said anything to him, he gave the guy a mean and evil glare.

"Are you okay? These niggas didn't fucking touch you, did they?" Gunner asked in concern as he placed his attention on his sister.

"I'm fine, no one did anything stupid; I'm just ready to go home," Kelsi answered as she sighed a sigh of relief. Deep down, she was happy and pleased to see Gunner and Latrell. But, she was ready to get far away from Cornell and all his madness.

"Good! Cornell, you better spend that hundred thousand dollars wisely and I mean that shit," Gunner said as he looked Cornell straight in the eyes. He didn't hide the disgust or hatred that he held in his heart. Everything that he was feeling in his heart was very clear on his face.

Gunner, Latrell, and Kelsi all turned around and walked towards the car. Once they reached the car, Gunner held the door open for Kelsi to get inside. Once she was inside, Gunner slid in right beside her.

"That's it? We can go now?" Kelsi asked as she looked between Gunner and Latrell, who hadn't got inside the car yet.

Before Kelsi could question anything else, she watched as Latrell held out two fingers in a gun motion, giving a signal. She knew exactly what that signal meant, and so did Cornell. Before Cornell could remove the gun from his hip, a number of rounds went off, hitting Cornell and the men standing with him.

Latrell quickly jumped in the car, started the engine, and pulled off. As soon as the gun shots went out, Gunner wrapped his arms around Kelsi and pulled her into his chest.

"It's all over now Kelsi, you're safe!" Gunner informed her, after placing a kiss on the top of her head.

6

I'm not trying to cause you any problems or pain, but I wanted to inform you about the people whom you have around. I'm not sure what all you know, or what all you believe. However, I know personally that your husband has been cheating. I have seen multiple times with the women in the picture or several different occasions. Again, I don't want to bring you any pain, but I couldn't sit back and allow you to look like a fool any longer...

As Amber read the letter for the hundredth time, the tears continued to fall from her eyes. She had read the letter and examined the photos every day since she opened the mail. She was looking for a reason to say it was all a lie, but there wasn't one. She was forced to deal with the news that her husband was cheating on her with his brother's girlfriend.

She wasn't sure what to say or what she should do from this point. She was numb to the pain. Every night, she cried until she couldn't cry any more.

It was getting to the point where she was blaming herself. Of course, there had to be signs that she overlooked, and all she could do was blame herself for being so naïve.

"Girl, you going to drive yourself crazy keep looking at that bullshit," Monica said as her and Daisy walked into the living room of her home.

"I say we just run up on his ass and beat the shit out of him," Daisy said, causing Monica and Amber to look at her like she was crazy. Amber shook her head from side to side and laughed to herself because she knew that Daisy was serious.

"All I'm saying is it will relieve some stress," Daisy said while shrugging her shoulders.

"So, we are not going to do anything crazy that could put us in jail," Monica said before taking a sip out of her wine glass.

"But no, seriously, what are you going to do from this point?"

"I'm not sure Daisy. I don't want to believe that he would do something like this to me, but I can't pretend that this information wasn't brought to me."

"Amber, don't be dumb. Yea, bitches lie and make up shit to break up your family. But, at the same time, no one is going to go through all these lengths for some lies," Daisy fussed.

"I agree Amber. Even if you don't want to believe the letter, the pictures should be enough to know what's really going on."

"I know. I just can't wrap my mind around how I was so dumb. Here I am telling this bitch my personal business and how I'm feeling about my husband, and her stupid ass sleeping with him."

"Just prove you can't trust a fucking soul. I told you it was a reason I never liked her ghetto ass," Daisy said with her face turned up while shaking her head.

"No, you haven't liked her since she spilled that drink on you that day," Monica said as she laughed to herself.

"So what. I still don't like her ass."

"I'm so damn naïve-" Amber started to say before she was cut off by Daisy.

No, you just very nice."

"I won't allow you to sit here and blame yourself. At the end of the day, Lakesha can be very manipulative. I have sat back and watched her sweet talk her way in and out of everything. Hell, it's been a few times where I had to take a step back and make sure I wasn't falling victim to her fucking ways," Monica added.

Monica may have been cool with Lakesha, but her loyalty lied with Amber. Amber introduced Lakesha to Monica and, from that point, she began to do Lakesha's hair. Over the years of doing her hair, the two began to talk and a friendship was formed. Monica never looked at Lakesha as a close friend, but they had a good working friendship.

"Plus, you're a damn good wife. You go to great lengths to make sure your husband and child is well taking care of. I have seen you make something out of nothing when it comes to him and your family. If he can't appreciate and love that about you, then clearly he does not deserve you," Daisy went on to argue.

"I hear you guys, I really do. I just don't know what else to do about this situation," Amber said truthfully.

"Do you think you will need real closure?" Monica asked. Before Amber was able to give her an answer, Daisy was already speaking.

"No, fuck that, do you feel like you need to speak face to face with whoever wrote you this letter. It's one thing to get a letter about this type of shit, but it's totally different when the information is coming face to face."

"I just want to make sure that the information is truly legit." No matter the proof that was sitting in her face or the weird behavior that was rushing to the fore front of her mind, she still needed more.

"Call the number that's at the bottom of the paper," Monica coached.

"You think I should?"

"Duh!" Daisy said as she picked up Amber phone and

handed it to her. Amber took a deep breath and removed the phone from her hands, before she unlocked the phone. Entering the numbers slowly, Amber couldn't believe she was about to go searching for additional answers that could further break her heart.

Hearing the phone ring, Amber placed the call on speaker and waited for someone to answer. The phone rung for a number of times, when Amber was about to end the call. However, just before her finger could connect with the end button, a female voice boomed through the phone.

"Hello."

"Hi, can I speak to Tina?" Amber asked in a very polite tone.

"This is she, who is this?"

"Hi, this is Amber. I received a letter from you," Amber said, hoping she didn't have to go into detail pertaining to what was in the letter.

"Oh yes, I'm sorry, how are you?"

"I'm fine. I was calling because I was wondering if you and I could sit and discuss the information in the letter you sent me."

"Sure, that's fine with me. I'm in my husband and I's restaurant, and I will be here for the next five hours. If you want to stop by, I'll be here," Tina informed.

"Where is the restaurant?"

"On 23rd street."

"That's fine. I'm not far from there. Give me about twenty minutes and I should be there then."

"That's fine," Tina said, causing Amber to end the call without saying anything additional.

"Come on, let's go get this over with," Daisy said before she threw the shot she was babysitting back and slammed the glass on the end table.

∼

AMBER SAT at the bar at the small, yet cozy restaurant. She was sitting with a glass of wine, while waiting for Tina to come out and meet with her. She may have been sitting by herself, but Daisy and Monica sat in a small booth nearby. They were not about to let their girl come meet with a stranger by herself.

"Hey girl, sorry, I was dealing with some staff issues in the back," Tina said as she approached Amber and walked around her to set in the chair beside her.

One thing Amber didn't like nor understand was why Tina was approaching her like they were cool. She came off so nice and nonchalant, like she didn't deliver heartbreaking news that destroyed everything she worked so hard to build.

"Um, you're fine," Amber said before taking a sip of her wine.

"So, I know you came here for a reason. So, we don't have to go through all the small talk. We might as well just cut to the chase," Tina said.

"That's fine with me. I wanted to meet because I received your letter, along with the pictures, in the mail; and I just had a few questions regarding them."

"Okay, I'm listening."

"Well, first of all, how did you know my husband?" Amber questioned.

"I don't, actually. I know Lakesha because her and my little sister is best friends. The two of them have been friends for years and my sister lives with me, so I can hear about all their gossip. A few months ago, they were in my living room and y'all situation came up. She was explaining how he invited her to a hotel because they couldn't do their dirt at hers any longer," Tina went on to explain.

"Being that she is your sister's best friend, why did you feel the need to bring this information to me?"

"Like I said, her and my sister are friends, but her and I are not. I don't like her and I never did. I deal with her off the strength of my sister, but that's as far as that goes."

"If you don't mind me asking, why?" Amber asked out of curiosity.

"Because she was fucking my husband. Her and my husband were sneaking around behind my back and fucking each other like rabbits. The only reason I found out was she started blackmailing him," Tina admitted.

"Wow!"

"Exactly, I never saw the signs nor was I out looking for them. In fact, I had this bitch up in my house treating her like the little sister I always thought of her as. But, in return, they both crossed me and had me out here looking like a fool. I was a fool and blind to it all so, if you don't have to be that same girl, then don't."

"And what was your outcome?"

"My husband and I have tried to save the marriage, but there wasn't no saving it. So, as of now, him and I finalized our divorce a couple months ago. My sister and I still working on our relationship, but that's a different topic for a different day," Tina further explained.

"I had an idea that the two of them were fooling around behind my back, but I truly didn't want to believe it."

"I understand that. I wasn't bringing the information to you so you can go through what I'm going through. However, after falling victim for her bullshit and dealing with it all firsthand, I believed that you should know."

"How did you get the pictures?"

"She left my house one day to go meet him, and I followed her. A few days later, I had to get the information out my sister on whom you were and how I could get in contact with you."

"Well, thank you for the information," Amber said as she was ready to end the conversation. She had all the information she needed, and there wasn't anything that Tina could say to make matters any better.

"You're welcome. Again, I'm not trying to hurt you or piss you off, but I felt that you needed to know what was being done behind your back. Especially since you and Lakesha are friends."

"I'm a firm believer that what's done in the dark will come to the light, so I really appreciate it," Amber said as she removed herself from the high-top bar chair.

Ending the conversation, Amber made her way in the direction of the exit door. There wasn't anything else that needed to be said between the two of them. After hearing everything that was said, Amber went from being sad to now just pissed and fed up. In this moment, she had made her mind up that she was done with Jamison. And the friendship she once had with Lakesha was done and over with for good.

7

Liquor bottles and smoking weed was all that kept Jamison halfway together as he paced the room, fighting to hold back the level of disappointment he felt for himself. He even took a few Norcos to get high enough to ease his mind. The pit of his stomach was tied in knots at the thought of what could have happened to his baby sister because of his greed to have money and power. Before his father's passing, he had a good heart. He sat and thought about how happier he was when his father was alive. Jason was the only person that could keep him grounded. And now he was a loose cannon that couldn't control the anger.

He was happy that Kelsi was at home and safe, but he couldn't bring himself to go and see her because he wasn't ready to face his family. He was ready to let Gunner have it if he said anything that pissed him off. It was bad enough that what he did was eating him alive.

He didn't need to hear how much of a fucked-up person he was from Gunner. He was more concerned with the fact that he made his mother cry. Maria had been through enough. He didn't want to be the son that always made matters worse. He couldn't look his mother or his sisters in the eyes. It hurt him to think that Kelsi would never forgive him.

Out of all his siblings, Kelsi was the one who always had his back, no matter what he was going through. She had love and compassion for anything that he believed in. There wasn't a time that he called her and she didn't answer or call him right back. He did the same for her. They had a bond that he knew was now broken.

The trap house was dark and cold; it almost seemed like it was lifeless. He wore his all red True Religion sweat suit, which he had on for the last two days. His appearance was no longer kept up. He hadn't thought about shaving since the day he heard about Kelsi's abduction. He hadn't eaten for hours and the hunger was making him sick, but he didn't have an appetite.

After pacing the room for what seemed like hours, he watched his phone as it lit up again and again, displaying Maria's house phone number. With each call, his heart became heavier. He picked his phone up off the desk that was in the corner and pushed it to silent. He wasn't ready to answer.

Taking time out in the trap house allowed him to think about all the people he'd done wrong over the last couple of years. He felt bad, but he wasn't sorry. The one thing he was apologetic for was hurting his wife. Amber was his world, but Lakesha threw the pussy at him anytime he wanted it and that gave him satisfaction. She showed him that he was that nigga. There was nothing he had to do to make her open the door for him whenever he needed to bust a quick nut. He didn't even have to respect her for her to give up the pussy.

Anytime Amber would go weeks without showing him love and affection, he would get that fulfillment from other women. But, he never wanted Amber to find out about Lakesha, of all the women he'd slept around on her with.

As he sat down in the hard-wooden chair that was next to the deck, he began going through his phone. He tapped his picture gallery and began scrolling through his pictures with one finger. He smiled as a single tear trickled down his cold cheeks and landed on his white tee-shirt. He was looking at pictures of Amber and Jamie. He missed his family and he was determined to keep them.

His moment was interrupted by the car door he heard slam outside. He stood up in a hurry and grabbed his gun from under his chair before he placed his phone into his pocket. He wasn't about to let no niggas think they could catch him slipping so he always kept his gun close to him. The way he was feeling, he was ready to spray anyone who thought about fucking with him. Today was not the day to test his crazy.

He made his way over to the window and pulled the blackout certain back far enough for him to see out, but no one could see in. His eyes lowered as he huffed.

Amber and Daisy had gotten out the car and was walking up to the door. Amber was in her pajama, the pink teddy bear matching set that he bought her two birthdays before. Her eyes were puffy like she hadn't got sleep in days. And to make her look even more out of line, she had on her robe.

By the look on Daisy's face, he knew that he was going to have to check her if she got out of line with him. He sighed and opened the door before she could knock. He wasn't ready for what she had to say, and he sure didn't want Daisy putting her two cents in their business.

When he first met Daisy, she seemed like a cool girl but, as he got to know her over the years, he realized that she was the one person that could make Amber act a damn fool. Daisy was always trying to fight, when Amber was the kind of woman that like to talk things through. Amber was sweet, and Daisy was a beast, especially when one of her loved ones was hurt. She always tried to talk shit to niggas because she knew that no one would hurt her, but Jamison wasn't the nigga that cared who she was or who her family was. He didn't want to hear nothing from Daisy and he was prepared to tell her that.

"What are you doing here?" Jamison asked as he swung the open the door.

He noticed she was carrying a manila envelope, so he shook his head. He knew that whatever was in the envelope was all bad. His first thoughts were that she was there to serve him with divorce papers, but he wasn't going to touch them. It was going to take more than some papers to get rid of him. His eyes were red from crying and he smelled like he'd been swimming in liquor.

"Where my daughter at?" Jamison added.

"She's with my mother for a few hours," Amber said before her and Daisy brushed passed him and made their way into the room.

"Why haven't you been answering my calls? You act like you don't have a wife and kid at home that needs you?" Amber continued to fuss as she stood there with her hand rested on her hip.

"I been busy with all that's been going on with my sister. I don't have time to argue with you, what's up?" he said as he stared down at the floor with his arms folded across his chest.

Amber looked over at Daisy, who stood firm with her arms to her side. She was dressed like she was ready to fight, wearing some sweats and a tee-shirt with her hair tied back into a ponytail.

"You would say that you're too busy to call your daughter," Amber questioned.

"I don't have time for you coming up to where I do my business talking shit to me. Just sit the divorce papers down and get on about your business. I'm not gone sit here and argue with you in front of your bodyguard."

"Who you are calling a bodyguard? I ain't never been a

bodyguard but, clearly, you been too busy protecting the next bitch, so somebody had to be here for Amber," Daisy snapped.

"Gone, Daisy. I'm not about to go there with you today. At the end of the day, you need to understand that my wife doesn't need no one to come with her to talk to me."

Daisy threw her hand up as she looked over at Amber, who was crying like someone had just cut her with a knife.

"Show him, Amber, so we can get out of here. This nigga makes me sick to my stomach," she said as she walked over and stood by the door.

"Show me what?" Jamison asked, as curiosity took over his mind.

"I know you lied to me about Lakesha," she sniffled. Amber wiped the snot off her nose with the back over her hand.

She pulled the copies of the pictures out of the envelope and handed them to Jamison. He began to flip through the pictures as he shook his head. There was nothing he could say because the proof was right in front of him.

"So, you got motherfuckers watching me?"

"Are you fucking serious?"

"Hell, yeah, you act like you're working for the police. How you gone have motherfuckers watching me and you know the lifestyle I live?"

"I would never have anyone watching you. Someone sent these pictures to me. I didn't ask for this pain."

"You are always playing the victim. Ain't no one going to go out their way to send you shit. I know you hired one of those private investigators to follow me around. You probably gave the police this address," Jamison snapped, with his entire demeanor changing in a matter of seconds.

"You are really trying to turn all this around on me. You know that I would never get the police involved in our life. I know what you do. I don't want my husband in jail," she assured him as a migraine formed in her head. She was crying heavier than she had cried since she got the pictures in the mail. The man she fell in love with was long gone. She didn't know who she was talking to and that scared her.

Jamison felt her pain like they had the same soul, but he didn't know how to go about fixing the situation because he knew he couldn't.

"I don't know what a bitch would do. All you bitches the same if you ask me," he said, trying not to show that he cared.

"So, now you're going to compare me to all those women you messed around on me with? I'm not only your wife, but you need to respect me as the mother of your child. I would never try to turn my shit around on you."

Jamison could no longer play the hard roll. He knew that if he kept on being an ass towards her, she would walk out of his life and he would no chance of making things right, but being caught up was making him mad.

"That's not what I'm saying baby."

"What are you saying?"

"I'm saying that I know I fucked up and I apologize. I wanted to tell you time and time again, but I didn't want you to leave me."

"But, why Lakesha out of all people?"

"I don't know, Amber. I really don't want to talk about this right now."

"It's not always about what you want. That's my problem; I have always given you what you want, but what about what I want? You never cared about my feelings!" she yelled as she got all up in his face.

"Back up and get your hands out my face," he said as he pushed her away from him.

"I hate you, Jamison. Why would you do this to me?" she cried as she charged towards him and began to hit him in the chest.

After taking hit after hit, Jamison was trying his hardest to get away from her. As soon as he attempted to turn to the side, Amber closed fist struck him in the jaw. Having enough of her shit, Jamison slapped Amber to the floor. He didn't do it intentionally, but his reaction became too hard to control.

Seeing her best friend hit the floor, Daisy rushed over to Amber, ready to help her friend by all cost. Daisy immediately stood in between both Amber and Jamison, in an attempt to get them both to stop.

"Jamison, stop hitting her!" she yelled.

"I can't believe you put your hands on me. You swore you would never do me like this," she said, as Daisy helped her off the floor.

"It's not like that baby, you know I didn't mean to hit you. You were going crazy on me, and I just... I just reacted."

"She doesn't want to hear none of that shit you're talking about. You know you fucked up and you want to put that shit off on her like she did something wrong. You need to man up and handle your shit!" Daisy roared.

"I'm not gone keep telling you to mind your business. You single bitches always try to play like you know everything about being in a relationship, but can't keep a man of your own."

Daisy walked up to him and got as close as she could get before saying what she had to say.

"I got your bitch, motherfucker. And when I see your bitch Lakesha, I got her ass too. You done tried to fuck over the wrong one."

"The way I'm feeling Daisy, it would be in your best interest to get the fuck out my face. I have too much pent-up anger, and the last thing you need is for me to take all that shit out on you. Now, you have three seconds to back your ass up before this shit get out of hand."

"Come on Daisy, let's go. I don't have time for this," Amber said as she got between them. One thing she knew for sure, Daisy wouldn't stand down from anyone. If this was a few months ago, Amber would have allowed for the situation to play out. However, because she didn't know the man who stood before her, she wasn't sure what he was capable of doing.

Daisy was stuck. She couldn't move. She wanted to hurt Jamison. One thing that bothered her was a nigga that thought he was untouchable. Those were the kind of niggas that she made sure got touched, but he was Jamie's father and Daisy didn't want her God baby to grow up without a dad.

"Come on Daisy. I need to get back to Jamie," she said once again before she looked over at Jamison. She knew how to make Daisy snap out of whatever she was thinking.

"Yeah, alright," Daisy said as she pinched her lips and followed behind Amber to the door.

Jamison allowed the two women to leave. He watched them drive off before he sat back down and made a phone call to Lakesha. When she didn't answer, he called her back, still no answer. He planned on calling until she picked up the phone. He didn't know who was behind sending pictures to Amber, but he was determined to find out. Whoever thought they could ruin his marriage was going to get it in the worse way.

AMBER SAT on her couch with an icepack pressed against her cheek. Jamison had slapped her so hard that he caused her beautiful face to swell and the black eye didn't do no justice to her busted lip. She had been home for hours before she called her mother to bring Jamie home. She didn't want her family to see her face like that, but she had no choice.

Jamie played around on her blanket that laid on the floor next to the coffee table. Amber watched and smiled at how much she looked like Jamison. She became angry at the thought that Jamison could have been spending time with his daughter, but he chose to spend time with Lakesha. Thinking about his infidelity made her want to get a divorce, but she loved her husband despite what he did.

Realizing that Jamie hadn't taken a bath, she swooped her up from the floor and cradled her to the back room. She took off her soiled onesie and ran a lukewarm bubble bath with less than an inch of water. Before she could place Jamie into the tub, her doorbell rang.

She wrapped a towel around Jamie and headed towards the front door.

"Who is it?" she asked, thinking that Daisy had forgotten something at her house.

"It's me, baby, open the door. I forgot my house key on my other key ring," Jamison said.

"I'm not opening the door Jamison. I think you need to leave," Amber said with her daughter on her hip and tears filling her eyes.

"Come on baby, let me talk to you. I know I fucked up and I can't change what happen, but you need to know that I am sorry. I don't want you to leave me. You and Jamie are my life. Please baby open the door."

Amber took a deep breath as she fought not to open the door. Jamison had hurt her time and time again, but the pain she felt when she opened the envelope that displayed the proof that he was messing around with Lakesha cut her deep. It hurt her more that she still wanted to make her marriage work.

"You need to leave right now. I'm not going to sit here and continue to listen to your lies. Haven't you hurt me enough?" She cried, as Jamie squirmed in her arms.

Jamison began to kick the front door as hard as he could. He wasn't going to leave his house without putting up a fight.

"I pay the fucking bills in this bitch, open this fucking door.

Jamie began to cry at the loudness that was being exchanged between both her parents. She was too young to understand what was going on, but she could sense that something wasn't right. Amber was scared because she had never seen Jamison behave like this before.

"Get away from the door or else I'm going to call the police."

"Back at the trap house you said that you would never call the police. Now, look at you- a police officer calling bitch. All they gone do is let me in. It's my house. My name is on all the paperwork, just like yours. So, do what the fuck you need to do," Jamison fussed.

"Goodbye, Jamison. Once you are calm and thinking straight, then I will allow you inside. But, until then, your daughter does not need to see you like this," Amber said in hopes that he would calmly walk away.

Before Jamison could put up a fuss, he noticed that the neighbor's light had come on and their nosey asses were peeking their head out the door. Not wanting to draw any more attention to the situation, he decided to say fuck it and let it go.

"You know what Amber, fuck you!" Jamison spat before walking away from his house. Amber watched from the window as he got in his car and sped off.

As much as she wanted to open the door for her husband and take him in her arms, she had to put her foot down. She needed to learn to love herself more than she loved her husband.

8

———

~ ONE WEEK LATER~

Kimberly: You need to get over here and see Kelsi. It is selfish of you to avoid her. You act like she did something wrong.

Jamison: Ima get over there soon, sis. I promise I been trying to work out how I'm going to look her in her eyes. I feel so bad about how all that shit went down.

Kimberly: Just get your black ass over here and see her. Stop being like that. Kelsi has been locked in her room since the day she got home. She needs you, J.

Jamison: Let me get up and wash my ass. I'll be over there in a couple of hours.

Jamison scratched his head before he pulled back the covers. He still felt like it wasn't time to face Kelsi, but it would never be the right time. He was never ready to hear his baby sister's cries or to feel her pain. A pain that could have been avoided.

He got out of bed one leg at a time and stood there looking at Amber sleeping. He was happy to be home with his wife and he wanted to spend every second with her so that she could know that he was serious about saving their marriage.

"Where you going?" Amber asked as she rolled over.

"I'm going to my mom house. Kimberly text me and told me that Kelsi wasn't doing good."

"You need to go over there. I think it's time."

"I was hoping that you would go with me. I don't want to face her by myself."

"Sure, I'll go with you," she said before she sat up and took a sip of the cup of water that laid on the nightstand beside her bed. She appreciated Jamison wanting her to support him.

"Thank you, baby. I don't know how I'm going to face Kelsi."

"It's not as hard as it seems. You know your sister loves you. All she wants you to do is show that you are apologetic for everything that happened."

"I am. I hate how broken my family is. I know it's mostly my fault, but Gunner sneaky ass did shit too. That nigga always plays the role like he doesn't do shit wrong and my mom falls for it every time. That shit makes me mad," Jamison fussed as he vented.

"You did have sex with his girl," Amber mentioned as she raised her eyebrows.

"Why you gone say some stupid shit like that?"

"Because it's true."

"Gone with all that shit, Amber. You act like you're fucking Gunner. You stay taking up for that nigga."

"I don't want to talk about it no more. Talking about it don't get us nowhere." Amber threw the covers to the side and got out of bed. She had been trying hard to put everything behind her, but she couldn't.

"You're the one that keep bringing the bitch up. From my understanding, Gunner don't fuck with her no more. I sure haven't seen or talk to her. But, you can't seem to let her ass go."

"What time are we leaving?" Amber asked while changing the subject. She threw up her hands before she slipped off her pajamas.

"Within the next hour. I want to hurry up and get this over with."

"Okay, let me take a shower and get Jamie ready."

"I can get Jamie ready while you're in the shower. I got this baby." He smiled.

Amber shot him a smile back as she grabbed her towel and some clothes. She was pleased at how he was treating her, but she couldn't love him like she wanted to. As she turned on the shower and waited for the water to heat up, she began to flip through her phone.

She had been getting missed calls from Daisy all week. She would call her back, but only to talk to her briefly. If she didn't call her back, then she would shoot her a text message and let her know that she would call her back. She couldn't let Daisy know that she let Jamison come back home. She knew that Daisy would go off if she told her.

She sat her phone down, took her panty and bra off, and hopped in the shower. As the hot water ran down her body, her thoughts began to rush all over her. She couldn't help but to think that she was forcing herself to be in a marriage that was tarnished.

She picked up her bath sponge and poured a generous amount of Dove bodywash onto it before she lathered it up and began to wash herself. The nerves in the pit of her stomach began to get the best of her. Her mind began to wonder about the last time she was happy. The one person that came to mind when she thought about that moment was Bruce.

"Come on in, y'all," Maria said as she opened the door with a smile on her face. She was happy to see Jamison and Amber, but Jamie melted her heart.

Amber and Jamison gave Maria a hug before Jamison handed her Jamie. Maria knew that Amber was aware of Jamison and Lakesha's infidelity and she could see the hurt in Amber's eyes.

"Hey, ma. How you been doing?"

"I been doing just fine, now that your sister is home," she responded, looking over at Amber. "How are you doing, Amber?" she asked.

"I'm here." Amber sighed, taking a seat on the end of the couch.

"Is Kelsi upstairs?" Jamison smacked his lips and rolled his eyes at her response. By this time, Jamison was sure his mother knew what was going on between the two of them, and the last thing he needed was a lecture for her.

"Gone on up there. She would love to see you," Maria said as she pointed to the staircase.

Maria and Amber sat on the couch and talked while Jamison made his way up the stairs. The walk to Kelsi's room seemed like it took forever. When he made it to her room, he stood there with his head held low. He couldn't bring himself to knock on the door.

He was about to turn around and walk back down the stairs when Kimberly came out her room door. The moment they saw one another, Kimberly jumped in surprise.

"Damn, Jamison, you scared me. What are you doing by Kelsi door?" she asked with her hand over her heart.

"I can't go in there, Kim. I know she hates me," Jamison honestly revealed.

"She might be disappointed and she might be hurt, but she

doesn't hate you," Kimberly said as she moved her hair out her face.

"I don't know what to say to her."

"How about saying, I love you and I apologize?" Kimberly whispered.

Jamison took a deep breath and knocked on the door.

"Come in," Kelsi said.

It warmed his heart to hear his sister's voice. He walked in, as Kelsi turned around to see who it was. The moment she saw who it was, she rolled her eyes and put her attention back on her phone. Kelsi rolling her eyes didn't go unnoticed to him, but he wanted to keep it cool and not make a big scene about it.

"Hey, Kelsi. I came by to see how you were doing."

"You see, now you can leave." Kelsi was sitting on her bed fully dressed in her black, pencil knee-length skirt and white blouse. She hadn't been to work, but she got dressed every day to make herself come out of the state of mind she was in. She was terrified to live a normal life around normal people because she knew what could happen to her.

"Come on lil sis. I know you are mad at me, but I need you to know that I am mad at myself. I know I fucked up and, if I were you, I would probably never talk to me again, but you and I are better than that.

"They almost killed me, Jamison, and you were nowhere to be found. You are so caught up in having the most money and being the nigga on the streets that you forgot about your family," she said with a saddened tone.

"I know, and I want to make it better. That's why I came over here to talk to you and let you know that I love you and I am so sorry for all that shit went down."

"What about Gunner?"

"Fuck Gunner! Gunner don't have nothing to do with me apologizing to you. He doesn't want to listen to me and I don't have shit to say to him," Jamison said as he took his phone out of his pocket to see who was calling him.

He stared at Lakesha's number on his missed calls list before he stuck his phone back into his pocket. He didn't bother to look at her text message because it wasn't important. Kelsi was important. He was there to repair the love he lost from his sister.

"Who is that calling you? It looks like you saw a ghost." Kelsi asked.

"That's not important. What's important is that I need you to forgive me for all this shit I got you in," he said.

Kelsi couldn't be mad at Jamison. He had been there for her through thick and thin. She rushed over to him and he swept her up in his arms, as they both shared the same hurt and love.

"I forgive you, Jamison. I'm just so scared to go outside."

"Don't be scared. I heard Gunner handled that already."

"He did, but there are more people like that where they came from. I don't know how to move on from here."

Jamison squeezed her tight, as she cried on his shoulder. Knowing that she felt like this caused him to feel even worse, because he was responsible for it all.

"One day at a time," he told her.

As they broke away from each other, they were shocked by the yelling and screaming from downstairs. Jamison was shocked when he heard Amber screaming at the top of her lungs, and Lakesha yelling just as loud.

"Awe, shit. That's Lakesha and Amber," Jamison said as he and Kelsi hurried down the stairs.

"Bitch, I'll kill you!" Amber roared.

"Bitch, bring it then with your scary ass." Lakesha fussed back.

Kimberly was standing in the middle of the two women, and Maria had taken Jamie into the room downstairs. She couldn't have her granddaughter in the same room with all the commotion that was going on.

"What are you doing here, Lakesha?" Jamison asked calmly as he approached him.

"I came to talk to Kimberly. I didn't know you were here until I pulled up and seen your car. That's why I called and texted you but, since you wanted to ignore me, I decided to come in," Lakesha admitted.

"Man, right now is not the right time to be here. You need to go on about your business," Jamison said, trying to diffuse the situation.

"Jamison, I hear everything that you saying, but I'm not here for you. If your insecure ass wife wants to cause problems, then she definitely barking up the right tree," Lakesha fussed.

Amber had enough. No one had noticed that she ran to the kitchen and grabbed the first big knife she saw. She was ready to cut Lakesha wide open for the pain she'd caused her.

"If you don't get out of my mother-in-law's house being disrespectful, I'm going to cut another hole in your ass. I have had enough of you," Amber assured Lakesha.

Lakesha looked at Kimberly and Kelsi, who wasn't saying a word. She was pissed off, true indeed, but she wouldn't dare let any of them see it.

"You think you all that because you got a knife. Bitch, you ain't shit and you not going to do anything with that shit."

Amber rushed passed everyone and began to swing her knife at Lakesha, barely missing her. Lakesha backed away a few steps to get away from the knife. If that knife wasn't in Amber's hand, then she would have beat her ass no doubt.

"Don't run now. I see you not talking all that shit!" Amber yelled in frustration.

"Amber, stop, you go end up in jail if you stab this girl. She not worth it!" Jamison yelled as he struggled to hold her back.

"Nah, fuck that. This bitch needs to feel all the pain that's coming her way. She thinks she can keep fucking with married men and everything going to be sweet," Amber continued to cuss and fuss.

"Man, calm your ass down!" Jamison yelled as he held her down on the couch and removed the knife from her hands. He didn't mean to use force with her but, in order to protect himself and everyone else in the house, he had too.

"Lakesha, please just go. This is my mother's house and right now is not the time for any of this shit!" Jamison yelled over his shoulder.

Both Amber and Jamison watched as Kimberly and Lakesha walk out the house. Over the past week that Jamison and Amber were back under one roof, she thought she could eventually forgive him and they would move on. However, after seeing Lakesha for the first time since the incident, she was forced to realize that she may not ever be able to move on from it.

9

"Ugh, I'm so fucking pissed off right now," Lakesha fussed as she let out her frustration.

"Seriously, you need to calm down," Kimberly said as she raised her eyebrow and held her hands out.

"When I called you earlier, why you didn't tell me she was here or that she was coming here? I wouldn't have brought my ass over if that wasn't the case, Kimberly."

"First off, I didn't even know that she was coming with him. I spoke to him earlier and made him come over here, but he never said anything about bringing his wife."

"Whatever, I'm just pissed right now," Lakesha admitted.

"And I get that, but disrespecting my mother's house is not cool at all," Kimberly said as she tilted her head to the side.

"That bitch came at me the moment I walked in that house."

"I never said she was right. Y'all both are in the wrong and both of you need to apologize to my mother."

You know what, your mother always been good to me. So, I can give you that, but I'm not saying shit to that bitch and I mean it," Lakesha said after taking a moment to think about the situation.

"Truthfully, I don't care what you and her do. All I ask is that y'all don't bring that to my mother's front door."

"You right."

"In other news though, what's up? What did you want to talk to me about?" Kimberly said, ready to change the topic

"Gunner."

"What about him?"

"I just don't know what to do from this point. He not answering my calls, my texts, or anything. He came by the house a few days ago and removed all of his belongings and left the key on the coffee table," Lakesha explained, causing Kimberly to look at her with a confused look. Kimberly wasn't sure what Lakesha expected, but she thought she was dumb to not think things would be the way they were.

"Lakesha, seriously, what do you expect? You acting like you wasn't fucking his brother while he was locked up."

"I expect him to hear me out and give me a chance to explain myself. He just went with the information that was told to him and didn't give me a chance to speak about it."

"You can't talk your way out of this one though."

"That's not what I'm trying to do but, at the same time, I expect to be giving a second chance. He cheated on me numerous times in the past and, yet, I forgave him."

"Maybe you need to give him some time to himself because none of this is making the situation better for you two. Give him his space to get his mind right, and see how things play out from there. However, you can't force him to forgive you and pretend nothing ever happened.

"You have a point."

"Let me ask you this though?" Kimberly asked in a calm voice.

"What's up?"

"What is your feeling towards Jamison?"

"Honestly... nothing," Lakesha said, telling a partial lie. A part of her didn't have feelings for Jamison, but there was another part that had some level of care and love for him.

"You sure?"

"Yea, things between Jamison and I weren't anything special. I was in a rough space with Gunner being gone. Jamison was there for me and making sure I was okay when I needed it the most. I acted off of emotions and didn't think about the consequences of my actions," she went on to explain.

"That's understandable but, at the same time, at this point, you just need to deal with your consequences. You can't point the finger at anyone but yourself."

"And I know that, which is why I was trying to speak to him about it."

"What is your feeling for Gunner now?" Kimberly asked, showing her curiosity.

"I love him and truly want to spend the rest of my life with him. Your brother means the world to me and, even though I fucked up, I wouldn't want to lose him for anything in this world."

"Okay, well, just give it some time."

"I don't have much time to be wasting. Plus, I think Gunner is fooling with someone else," Lakesha continued to vent.

"What makes you think that?"

"This may sound crazy and all, but I followed him one day he left the house. Him and some female went out and, from the looks of it, it seemed like they were all cozy with each other."

"What's her name?" Kimberly asked with her eyes squinted.

"Something like Toni, I believe." Lakesha knew what her name was for sure but chose to pretend as if she wasn't sure.

"Yea, that doesn't sound familiar."

"I don't know who the chick is, but I'm not cool with the situation regardless."

"Okay, well, I'll talk to him and see what that is about," Kimberly said, knowing that she wasn't taking the information back to her. She was only going to question Gunner, so she could be nosey.

"Bet! Let me get up out of here though before Amber do something to get her ass beat," Lakesha said as she shook her head from side to side.

"Okay," Kimberly said before the two of them walked away from one another.

Kimberly didn't have a major problem with Lakesha, but she couldn't respect the moves she made. Lakesha could give excuse after excuse, but it meant nothing to her because she could see through the lies. Kimberly prayed that Gunner was able to see through Lakesha's bullshit once and for all.

"So, how is everything with your family?" Toni asked, as Gunner gave her his undivided attention via their facetime call.

"Everything coming together. Seems like things are going back to normal," Gunner answered.

"That's good. I'm happy to hear that your sister is back home and you know she is safe."

"Yea, I don't think she went back to work yet, but we getting there. Enough about that though, how is everything on your end?" Gunner asked while shifting the conversation. The mention of the things she was going through at the moment caused her attitude to go from happy to annoyed.

"It is what it is at this point," Toni said after a deep sigh.

"You haven't spoken to your sister yet?"

"Not really, she called late last night looking to speak to Mario. I didn't even bother to entertain her stupid ass because she knew good and well that he was sleep," Toni explained while rolling her eyes.

Toni was very much fed up with her sister and the shit she was doing. After dropping her son off without notice, you would think her sister would check up on him or come back to get him. But, there was nothing. She would call every now and then, but that wasn't good enough for Toni. She just couldn't understand how a mother could do this to her own flesh and blood.

"Did you at least ask when she was coming back to get him or if she was?"

"Nope! I asked her where she was and she told me that she was with her new boyfriend. I know her enough to know that whoever she with is not someone Mario should be around. She not welcomed in my house so, for her sake, she better stay the fuck away."

"I understand what you saying. However, you have to remember that she is his mother and she does have rights to him. You can't just keep him away from her because he may resent you in the future," Gunner explained, trying to get Toni to look at the situation from a different pair of eyes.

"I know, but I want to do everything I can to protect him. I'm just not sure what to do any more. I'm tired of her and her shit but, at the same time, I look out for her because she is Mario's mother," Toni said.

"And your sister..." Gunner added while allowing his words to trail off.

"Yea, that as well."

Silence fell over Toni and Gunner, as Gunner starred at Toni while biting down on his bottom lip. Instead of saying anything, Toni sat there and blushed. The stare down between them was interrupted by a loud noise in Toni's background.

"Hold on... Mario, stop playing with your food. If you don't eat your vegetable, you not getting any ice cream and cake," Toni fussed as she took her attention from the phone call to where Mario was sitting.

"Mario, don't believe the hype. Feed them peas to the dog and get your desert!" Gunner called out while laughing.

"Gunner, shut your ass up! The last time you told him to do something, he actually did it," Toni fussed while turning her attention back to the call.

"Oh yea, that what your ass gets," Gunner continued to joke.

"Whatever. Did I tell you I will be near that way tomorrow?" Toni said.

Before Gunner could respond to Toni, his attention was briefly interrupted by Latrell getting back into the car. After taking the bag, which contained his food, he returned his attention back to Toni.

"No, you didn't. But, what you coming this way for?"

"Going to see my father," Toni answered.

"Cool, tell him I said what's up when you do see him."

"I will!"

"What you doing afterwards?" Gunner asked while running his tongue over his bottom lip.

"Um, I have nothing planned."

"When you going to let me take you out?" Gunner questioned.

Since ending everything with Lakesha and removing his belongings from their house, Gunner was now a single man. Even though he wasn't going to rush into anything, he wasn't going to sit back and be sad about the shit they had going on.

"Excuse me?"

"Your smart ass heard me."

"I don't be having time for personal outings. It's bad enough you force breakfast meetings on me once a damn month," Toni said while trying to play hard to get.

"You just said you don't have anything planned afterwards, so what's the problem now?" Gunner asked while using her own words against her.

"I'll think about taking you up on that date offer."

"Yea, okay. Well, go ahead and finish up whatever it is that you were doing; I'll hit your line later."

"Okay," Toni said before the two of them ended the call. Gunner couldn't hide from the smirk on Latrell's face.

"What the fuck your ass looking and smirking at?"

"Nothing... nothing at all," Latrell said as he shook his head and chuckled to himself.

"Nah, say what's on your chest," Gunner advised.

"That girl got your ass blushing and showing all thirty-two of your teeth."

"It's not even like that," Gunner said, causing him to blush even more.

"If that helps you sleep at night, then whatever you say."

"I swear..."

"All I'm saying is don't rush into anything until you close that chapter with Lakesha first. You can say one thing now regarding that situation, but the breakup is still fresh. Isn't any telling how that shit going to play out in the future," Latrell said.

"On the real bro, I don't see myself ever forgiving Lakesha and Jamison for the trifling shit they did. They can spit a bunch of bullshit to me about the matter, but that shit won't mean anything," Gunner admitted.

"I feel you but, at the same time, I would move slow with Toni. Don't hurt her in the process or use her as a rebound because that shit didn't work out."

"Understood," Gunner said, allowing the conversation to end.

10

Toni sat in the cold metal chair and tapped her fingers on the cold table. Every time she came to visit Santana, her nerves always got the best of her. She loved her father dearly, and seeing him locked up in shackles always broke her heart.

Toni watched from the chair she was sitting in, as her father and the other inmates approached the visitor's area. A big smile crept across her face as she saw how nice and healthy he looked. One of her biggest fears was that her father would have been mistreated while serving his time. However, it was no secret that Santana ran things throughout the prison, so he didn't have to expect any bullshit coming his way.

After being checked and allowed to proceed, Santana immediately made his way to his daughter. As he approached the table with a big grin, he wrapped his arms tightly around his baby. The two of them stood there holding each other for minutes, before they pulled apart from each other and took a seat at the table.

"How are you doing baby girl?" Santana questioned.

"I'm good! How are you doing in here?"

"Everything is everything. I'm about ready to get up out this bitch, I know that for sure."

"Did they say anything about when that may be?" Toni asked, hoping that he could give her some good advice.

"My lawyer just keeps saying soon but, shit, there isn't any telling on when soon will be. He doesn't want to put a date on anything and get my hopes up, only for something to happen and that shit not fall through," Santana explained.

"I know, I know. He called me a few days ago and gave me an update on what to expect your next court date."

"That's what's up. Just do everything he ask of you, and we can pray for a better outcome for the situation."

"I am," Toni said before taking a deep breath.

"Well, how is everything else going down on your end?"

"Well, business is booming and numbers are going way up."

"Oh really..." Santana said in disbelief while allowing his words to trail off.

"Yea, I went over the numbers and compared them from a two months' time, and the numbers increased drastically."

"What is it that you are doing differently in the last couple months?"

"Well, you know I added someone new to the team. That counts for most of the increase," Toni admitted.

"G?" Santana asked for clarification while using the nickname he had for Gunner.

"Yea."

"How is that working out?"

"Really good. I didn't expect for things to be doing so good so fast but, I guess when there's a need, you have to fill it," Toni explained while shrugging her shoulder.

"Let the work speak for itself. If you confident in what you selling, then everything will play itself out," Santana said in a low tone.

"Oh yea, Gunner did tell me to tell you he said hi."

"I know, I received his letter today."

"He made it seem to me like the two of y'all haven't talked since he left," Toni said with her lips pressed together.

"Maybe because he doesn't want you to know that we were discussing you," Santana said with his eyebrows lifted.

"Oh really? What about me? I hope it was all good things."

"It's good... I guess," Santana said with a small laugh to himself. Everything that Gunner said to him really pertained to business, but he wanted Toni's mind to wonder.

"You playing way too much pops," Toni said while laughing and calling his bluff.

"I'm just playing; he just told me that you be playing hard to get," Santana revealed, causing Toni to look at him through squinted eyes.

"Wait, what? Why would he even think it's okay to talk to you about that? Also, I'm not playing hard to get, I just haven't gone on a date with him."

"Why not?" Santana asked out of curiosity.

"All business, never personal," Toni answered with her favorite life motto.

"Your mother and I mixed business and personal together and we have been perfectly fine with one another," Santana said.

"You and mommy were different. The two of you started dating way before you got in the business. She had no choice but to support and stand by your side."

"I hear what you saying, but what is one date going to hurt?"

"You really like him, huh?" Toni asked with a smirk on her face. Santana had never entertained any conversation with her about a man, until now.

"Yes! Gunner is a good guy; he just very much like you. You two are very self-less and you two put your all into other people. That could be a very good thing but, at the same time, it could be bad because people take advantage of that," Santana explained.

"Yea, I can see that."

"All I'm saying is take him on that offer and go out and enjoy yourself. You never know what the outcome could be."

"Okay, and if it's bad, then I will be the first to complain to you," Toni said with her lips pressed together and her head tilted to the side.

"And I'll be the first to bust a cap in his ass," Santana said just above a whisper, causing himself and Toni to laugh.

Toni pulled up to the address Gunner had sent her via text, only to find that it was an apartment complex. Here she was wearing a tight Gold dress that hugged each and every one of her curves. The six-inch black heels she wore as well added to her height and also made her legs appear longer than they were.

Not wanting to get upset, she picked her phone up from the console and dialed Gunner's number. While she waited for an answer, she looked around the neighborhood and was impressed with the things she saw. It was eight at night and people were out walking their dogs.

"Yea," Gunner said as soon as he answered the phone.

"I'm at an apartment complex, am I at the correct place?" Toni questioned.

"Yea... park your car and come up. When you get to the door, hit the buzzer for 804 and I will buzz you in," Gunner instructed as he watched her from the window of his new apartment.

Toni did as she was told and, once she entered the building, she immediately walked towards the elevators. While riding the elevator up to the eighth floor, she checked her phone for any text messages or emails she could have missed. Once the elevator doors open, she approached the door and rang the doorbell while waiting for an answer.

"Hey," Gunner said as he opened the door and stood to the side for her to come in.

"Hey," Toni said as she entered his neatly decorated apartment. The smell of seafood filled her nostrils, causing her hunger to increase. What she thought was going to be a fun night out on the town, was clearly turning into a night in.

"You look beautiful," Gunner complimented, causing Toni to blush.

"You look very handsome yourself," Toni complimented back after taking a moment to look over his outfit. Gunner wore a nice pair of black khaki pants, with an Armani Black, white and grey ombre button-up shirt. On his feet, he wore a fresh pair of Prada tennis shoes. He wasn't too dressy, but his jewelry and swag alone made him look extra special.

"Thank you! Follow me, I already have dinner set up," Gunner said as he held his hand out for her to take.

"Oh, we staying inside?" Toni asked for clarification.

"Yea... is that okay with you? I know you were saying you was tired earlier, so I assumed you would have rather stay in and chill."

"It's perfectly fine, I just didn't think you were the cooking type of man."

"Really? Girl, I love cooking, it's something I like to do from time to time to ease my stress," Gunner said as he dramatically acted like he was shocked. It wasn't the first time a female told him he didn't seem like the cooking type, and he never understood why.

"Truthfully, I wouldn't have guessed that."

"See, it's a lot you don't know about me."

"Mhm!" Toni said, causing them both to chuckle, while taking his hand in hers.

Gunner led Toni to the dining room, where he had the floor decorated with rose petals. On the table was a scented candle, two plates, and two wine glasses. As Toni overlooked the room, a satisfying smile crept on her face. She had never had a guy do anything this romantic for her, and she appreciated it.

For the next forty-five minutes, Gunner and Toni sat at the table, ate dinner, and enjoyed conversation with one another. Toni was seeing a different side of Gunner over dinner and the side of him she was seeing she was satisfied with. She came to dinner thinking she would have been counting down the time until the end but, surprisingly, that wasn't the case.

"Seriously Gunner, this food is fucking amazing," Toni said as she ate the last of her lobster.

"Thank you, I'm happy you enjoyed it," Gunner replied with a smile on his face. He knew his food was good, but he enjoyed when others complimented the dishes he cooked.

"I did, actually. Have you ever thought about taking cooking serious?"

"Not really," Gunner truthfully answered with his face scrunched up.

"What? What the hell, why not?" Toni asked, showing that she was surprised that he wasn't taking advantage of the talent he had.

"I been hustling since a youngin, I haven't giving thought to anything else," Gunner answered.

"It's different types of hustling. Don't limit yourself to one thing. True, there's always people out here getting high, but you have to think about your future. Later in life, what you going to do, leave your kids with a pound of work and tell them go make money? At some point, you have to break the cycle," Toni informed, giving her advice on the matter.

"I never thought about it like that, honestly. My pops taught me how to make get rich from the drug game, and that's all I been sticking with. Once he got sick, it was like fuck it, I had to make ends meet the best way I knew how."

"Believe me, I understand that."

"You taking your own advice?" Gunner questioned with his eyebrow raised.

"Have you ever heard of Santos Real Estate?"

"I've seen a couple ads."

"Yea, well, that's my real estate company. Before my father caught his bid, I went to get my real estate license. Since then, I started a real estate company, and we have been providing services all over the Florida state. I was never supposed to get in the game but, clearly, life happened," Toni went on to explain.

"Your father never mentioned any of that to me."

"I don't think my father truly knows how big my company is now. He truly only knows what I tell him because he was never out when I opened everything."

"Yea, well, I'm sure if he knew the specifics, he would be very proud."

"Speaking of my father, why didn't you tell me you two have been talking?" Toni questioned as the conversation she had with her father came to her mind.

"I didn't know I had to run that by you," Gunner said, being smart.

"I mean... you don't have to but, at the same time, you had me exchanging messages like you haven't."

"Nah, him and I only talk through letters," Gunner informed with a small laugh.

"Yea, okay."

"I'm serious."

Following those words, Gunner and Toni sat there trapped in their own thoughts in silence. Gunner sat across the table with a smile on his face and just stared at Toni. Just like Toni was enjoying her night, so was Gunner. He was able to get his mind off the shit he had going on and just enjoy the moment he was in. He couldn't have asked for a better night from her.

"On another note though, I want to thank you for allowing me to have some of your time and attention tonight," Gunner said while speaking up.

"You're welcome. Also, thank you for making tonight a good night; I truly enjoyed myself."

"As long as you happy, then that's all that matters," Gunner said.

Toni chuckled to herself while looking at Gunner. So many things were running through her mind in this moment.

"Why you looking at me like that?" he added after a brief pause.

"No reason," Toni said after looking away.

"Nah, speak whatever is on your mind," Gunner encouraged.

"You have made me a very special woman tonight. I'm just trying to figure out what flaws that you have that would cause a female to cheat," Toni said as she shook her head from side to side.

"Sometimes, it's not what the one person is doing or not doing, it could just be a situation where the person who cheated has their own fucked up problems," Gunner answered.

"I'm sorry, you're right," Toni said as she chuckled. She felt foolish after those words left her mouth and she actually thought about what she was saying.

"Your good, no need to apologize," Gunner said with a small smile on his face. He wasn't offended by what Toni said because those thoughts ran across his mind a few times.

The conversation continued between the two of them a little longer, before they stood from their seat and began to clean the table. While Gunner removed the dishes from the dining room and placed them in the sink, Toni rinsed them and placed them in the dish washer.

"You not going to move?"

"No,"

"Well, do something then," Toni said, not thinking that Gunner was going to kiss her lips.

As their lips connected, Gunner pulled Toni closer to him and wrapped his arms around her waist. With his hands caressing her butt, their kisses went from a few small pecks to more passionate kissing. Toni wrapped her arms around Gunner's neck and pressed her body into him.

'Let's stop," Gunner said as he pulled back from her a little.

"No, I don't want you to," Toni said as she looked into his eyes and bit down on her bottom lip.

"You sure?" Gunner questioned.

"Yes," Toni answered.

Before making any move, Gunner paused and looked Toni in the eyes before lifting her up and placing her on the table. Gunner placed more kisses on Toni's lips, before proceeding down to her neck. He slid the gold straps off her shoulders and slowly pushed her dress down. Once her double D breasts were revealed, he took one in his hand and ran his finger over her nipple.

Toni threw her head back, as Gunner took the breast he was holding and placed it in his mouth. Gunner sucked and licked all over both of Toni's breasts, causing Toni to moan out loud.

Once he was done, he continued to work his way down while pushing the dress down as well. After having the dress completely off Toni, he pushed her down on the table so that she was lying on her back. Placing her legs on his shoulders, he came face to face with Toni's sexy pussy.

Running his tongue across his lips, he was ready to devour what was in front of him. Not wanting to waste another moment, he ran his tongue over her already wet pussy. Gunner began to suck on her clitoris, which Toni enjoyed.

"Damn," Toni moaned as she placed her hand on the back of his head.

Gunner continued to eat her pussy until her legs began to shake. As her legs began to shake uncontrollably, she started pushing Gunner's head back. Typically, Gunner wouldn't have stopped and just slapped her hands away but, this time, he chose to go against that.

"You okay?" Gunner asked as he stood up to his full height.

"Yea," Toni answered as she tried to catch her breath. Before saying anything else, Gunner removed his shirt and the rest of his clothes. Revealing his dick, Toni looked down with anticipation. Toni had never seen a dick so long, fat, and pretty. Even the curve that he had was pretty damn perfect to her.

Gunner picked Toni up from the table and carried her to the living room and placed her body on the couch. Although he laid her on her back, Toni wasted no time flipping around and being on all fours.

Gunner slid his hard dick into her wet tunnel from the back and grabbed ahold of her waist. Toni tensed her body up because she wasn't used to someone his size, causing Gunner to slow stroke her.

"Relax and take this dick ma," Gunner coached as he placed a kiss on the middle of her back. Although Gunner like to have slow passionate sex on occasions, in this moment, he wasn't feeling that. He had too much pent-up aggression stored up and he wanted to hardcore fuck.

Gunner placed his hand on the back of her neck while keeping hold of her waist. Not fooling around any longer, Gunner started giving her hard-back shots.

"Shittttt!" Toni moaned.

"You like this shit, huh?"

"Yes Papi, yes!" Toni screamed out loud as she continued to take Gunner's dick.

"Good!" Gunner said while he continued to pound into Toni.

The two of them continued to have sex for an additional forty minutes before Gunner and Toni both had an orgasm. Both Gunner and Toni laid down on the couch to catch their breath before getting up and walking to his bedroom.

11

D ave sat in the passenger seat of Tay's car. He had just received the news that Cornell was killed and his heart was broken into a million pieces. Dave and Cornell had a close relationship, a relationship that Dave would forever be happy for.

"I can't believe this shit!" Dave said as he laid his head back and closed his eyes. A single tear escaped his eyes as the thoughts of his favorite cousin crossed his mind.

"I know man. That shit happened so fucking fast that no one expected that shit to go down like that," Tay admitted.

"How y'all let him go out like that?" Dave asked as he shook his head from side to side.

"We didn't allow shit to go down any kind of way. He told me to fall back and dip because I was about to fuck them other little niggas up. But, not even just that. I don't think he expected any of this shit," Tay informed while also being a little offended.

"That nigga Jamison not even like that-" Dave said before Tay cut him off mid-sentence.

"Who?"

"What you mean who?"

"That name, it sound familiar," Tay said as he pulled on his chin hair and squinted his eyes.

"Because that's who he was meeting that night."

"From what I was told from Benny, he met with a nigga name Gunner."

"How though? I was with him when he got the fucking text from Jamison. I even called Jamison and he told me he was busy handling some personal shit," Dave questioned while being very confused.

"Either he was handling some other shit, or he was just lying to you. However, Benny the only one survived that shit, so I'm taking his word on it."

Benny was one of the guards that Cornell had on payroll. Benny was like an uncle to Cornell. He had been a friend of their family for years now and Cornell trusted him with his life. Following the shooting, Benny was the only surviving victim. Although he was now bound to a wheelchair, he survived, which meant the most to him.

"I'm fucking mind blown."

"Regardless though, we have to do something about this shit. I can't just let this shit slide," Tay said as he watched the cars pass them by.

"Why? What else happened?" Dave asked as he turned his attention to him.

"The bitch we kidnapped knows my damn name. Them niggas I was with didn't know what the fuck to do. They had they face mask off, dropping names, really just being fucking stupid," Tay explained.

"I told Cornell way back before that he needed to stop dealing with their asses. Them niggas was getting too comfortable and letting their guard down like they couldn't get touched."

"Yea, well, I'm not trying to have shorty remember some

shit; then, I have a target on my back. I rather get them niggas before they try and get me."

"I feel you! I'm getting revenge for Cornell death and I'm getting it by any means," Dave said as he took a deep breath.

"I'm down with whatever!" Tay snapped.

"Bet, say no more."

~THREE MONTHS LATER~

Gunner stood in the bathroom looking into the mirror while brushing his perfectly straight teeth. He was searching for some kind of answers but couldn't seem to come up with a reason why Jamison would want to have a meeting with him.

At first, he wasn't going to meet with him. When Jamison promised that he wouldn't be on no bullshit, Gunner agreed to hear him out. He missed his brother. And he wanted to show his mother that he and Jamison could actually be in the same room without trying to tear each other's head off.

"What are you doing in there, baby?" Toni asked.

He spit the remains of his toothpaste in the bathroom sink before he rinsed his mouth.

"I was brushing my teeth. You act like you miss me already," he said, before walking out the bathroom and staring at her lying in his bed.

"Don't flatter yourself." Toni shot at him with a smile.

"I know you ain't talking shit," he said playfully. Gunner climbed on top of her as they began to kiss.

"That's what I do."

"Is that right?"

"You know that's right, big daddy."

Their conversation was interrupted by his phone ringing. Gunner grinned at Toni calling him daddy as he arose from between her legs. He walked over to the nightstand where his phone was and reached for it. Toni watched him. She always watched him as he walked away from her. She was intrigued by his built body and his sexy swag. She knew that Gunner was who she wanted to spend all her time with, but he never talked about the status of their relationship, so neither did she.

Gunner frowned his face when he saw that it was Lakesha calling him. He didn't want to talk to her. He glanced over at Toni as he slid the call to ignore. He wanted Lakesha as far away from his memory as she could get her.

"Why you look at me like that, baby?"

"Nothing," Toni said, not wanting to seem curious.

"That was Lakesha calling me again. That girl just don't get that I've moved on."

"Did you really move on?"

"You know I did. All I do is think about you."

"I know you do... but."

"But, nothing. I told you that I don't ever want to fuck with that bitch again. The way she hurt me is unforgiveable. I was a real man to her and I was all in until she crossed me. What part of that don't you understand?"

Toni got out of bed and walked over to Gunner. She was sick and tired of talking about Lakesha. She wanted to make sure that Gunner knew she appreciated him. She pressed her body against his as she stared up at him, as she smiled at him staring down at her.

"Let's not argue about her anymore. I know how bad she hurt you, so we need to put that woman and all her issues behind us."

"Now, that's what I'm talking about," Gunner said as he smacked her on her ass.

"What do you got planned for today?" Toni grinned.

"I got to check on that last shipment but, before I do that, I'm going to talk to Jamison. He seem like he is getting his mind right, so I'm going to give him a chance to say what's on his mind."

Reaching up to rub his ears, Toni looked him in his eyes. She knew how it felt to argue with a family member and she didn't like the feeling.

"I'm happy y'all gone finally have a talk. I wish my sister would come to her senses and grow the fuck up. That girl get on my nerves. She don't seem to understand nor appreciate when someone is helping her."

"She'll come around one day. You just have to give it some time."

Toni didn't respond. She pinched her lips and walked out the room. There was no way that she was going to have a conversation about her sister. Just the thought of her made her mad.

"You want some breakfast?" she asked, yelling from the kitchen.

"Nawl, my mom made breakfast. I'm going to eat with her, but you can make me some steak and shrimp for dinner," he said as he made his way to the closet to grab some clothes. "You want to come?"

"You know your sister, Kimberly, might not like me."

Gunner lowered his eyes as he watched Toni walk back into the room.

"Why you say that?"

"Because she is friends with Lakesha."

"Damn, Toni. I don't want to keep hearing about Lakesha every second of the day. My sisters are not like that. They like anyone who makes me happy. That's on you if you don't take the time to get to know them."

"Whatever Mr. Brown. Tell everyone I said hello."

"I surely will," he responded as he slipped on his clothes and grabbed his keys.

"Good morning son," Maria greeted Gunner.

She was still in her oversized nightgown that she'd worn for the last ten years. The house smelled like a restaurant. Gunner was hungry, but his nerves had gotten the best of him. He had already made up in is mind that if Jamison try to beast up on him this time, he would not ever try to make things right with him.

"It smells good in here. I hope you saved some for me."

"You know I did. Come on in here and get you something to eat."

Gunner walked into the kitchen and began to smile at Jamison, Jessica, Kelsi, and Kimberly having a debate at the table. It reminded him of when they were kids before their father passed.

"What are y'all fussing about now?" He giggled.

"Jamison gone sit up here and tell me that pork ain't bad for you." Kelsi said, being the first to speak up.

"It ain't. Pork makes me happy. I don't ever plan on giving it up." Jamison laughed.

Gunner looked at Jamison and back at Kelsi before responding. "It's bad for you. I don't eat pork at all."

"Pass me the pork, please!" Kimberly chuckled.

"Now, that's what I like to hear." Jamison handed Kimberly the plate of crispy bacon.

They all sat and shared a laugh, as Gunner sat down at the table next to Jamison where the empty plate was. He sat there in silence and watched everyone talk and laugh as tears escaped from his eyes.

"What's wrong, brother?" Noticing that Gunner had tears falling from his eyes, Kelsi spoke up causing everyone else to stop talking.

Maria had walked into the kitchen to pour her a tall glass of orange juice. The moment she noticed tears in Gunner's eyes, she began to cry with him. She felt whatever it was that he was feeling and she wasn't sad. She was happy to have all of her children sitting at the breakfast table, but she wished Joe was there to see how beautiful his family was.

Gunner took a napkin and wiped both sides of his mouth.

"I missed so much when I was locked up. But, the thought of eating breakfast without you here Kelsi is killing me. I'm am so happy you are safe."

Jamison became teary eyed and so did Kimberly. He hated that he couldn't save Kelsi, but he was thankful that Gunner was there for him when he needed him.

"Thank you," Jamison said to Gunner.

"For what?" Gunner asked.

"For being the loyal brother that you always were. I know I messed up in the past, but you know that I'm not the kind of person. I just got so caught up in the money. When I started making money, people did whatever I said. That is what made me feel like I didn't need no one." He cried.

"You're welcome. I want you to know that I love all of you and I will always be here to support you with anything that you want to do in life, as long as your life is not in danger." Gunner said as tears continued to roll down his face.

"Y'all need to stop. Y'all got me over here crying," Kimberly said.

"Me too," Kelsi sniffled.

"Me three," Jessica added.

Maria let her children have their moment. She made her

way back into her bedroom and turned on her tv. She was proud that Jamison and Gunner were bonding. A weight was lifted off her heart when she heard them talking.

After they finished eating, Kelsi, Jessica, and Kimberly went into Kelsi's bedroom to give Gunner and Jamison some time to have a much-needed conversation. The girls were happy that the men they loved the most were finally able to be in the same room without trying to kill each other.

"What did you want to talk to me about?" Gunner asked as the two men sat on separate couches.

Jamison grabbed the remote off the arm of the couch and turned the TV to ESPN. He had to think carefully about what he wanted to say first and how he was going to say it.

"Amber don't want me no more. This time, I fucked up big time. I don't think she'll ever forgive me," he said as he let out a hard sigh.

"You just have to give her some time. When she saw those pictures of you and Lakesha, she nearly killed that woman."

"I know. Also, I just wanted to apologize to you as well. I was wrong, and I knew I was in the fucking wrong. If you never forgive me for that shit, then I can't do anything but understand that."

"I forgive you, Bro. I had to come to the realization that her and I weren't meant to be together anyway. I can't speak for Amber, but I know how much you mean to her. Where is she at anyway?"

"She won't tell me. She took Jamie and left. All I can do is call her. She won't let me see her. This shit is killing me."

"You just got to take it one day at a time. Trust is everything, so you are going to have to rebuild that with the people."

"I'm a real fuck up, huh?" Jamison scratched his head while he laughed.

"Yeah, you a fuck up." Gunner laughed as he grabbed a

pillow and threw it at Jamison, hitting him in his head. "You need to have a drink and chill out," Gunner added.

"I'm drinking if you're buying, rich guy." Jamison said as he playfully threw the pillow back at Gunner, but he missed.

"Grab my keys. Let's go for a ride."

Jamison grabbed Gunner's keys off the kitchen table as the two of them headed out the front door. As they hopped in the car, Jamison smiled at how clean Gunner's car was. He knew by the look of his all white Benz that Gunner was doing good.

The two of them rode in the car and talked for a few minutes. They hadn't had time to see what was up with one another. Jamison wanted to pick his brain about his connect, but he didn't want Gunner to question his motives.

"So, I heard you got a new girl," Jamison said, looking in the side mirror at the all neon Buick that was getting closer.

"She not my girl. We're taking it slow right now. I don't want to rush things with her."

"Are you hitting that every night?"

"Get out my business." Gunner laughed.

"Yeah, you hitting that," Jamison chuckled.

"Do you see that Buick behind us?" Gunner asked as he began to sped up.

"Yeah, I was tripping off that. It's been behind us for a minute now. Turn down this alley." Jamison responded.

Gunner made a left turn in the back alley on Drexel Avenue. His heart began to race when the Buick turned too.

"Awe shit. That's them niggas that took Kel-"

Gunner couldn't get a word out as a shot fired, breaking his back window. He slammed his foot on the gas and made it to the end of the alley onto a back street. Jamison had already taken out his pistol and began to shoot at the car.

"Drive this motherfucker, Gunner. Them niggas got hella guns!" he screamed as he continued to aim at the car.

"I'm driving. You just make sure you get a good shot."

The men in the car continued to shoot as Jamison focused on them. He tried with all he had to make sure that none of the bullets got near Gunner, but the Buick wasn't slowing down. It sped fast enough to touch Gunner's bumper.

Jamison saw who it was plain as day. He frowned and took his last shot before he was yanked back from the car, crashing into a pole. With the horn blowing, Jamison managed to get up.

"Gunner!" He cried as he pulled his brother from the steering wheel. His eyes widened at the shock of blood gushing from Gunner's back, barely missing his neck.

"Come on bro, don't die on me. Gunner! Gunner!" he called out as loud as he could, shaking with every word.

Hysterically, Jamison took his shirt off and pressed it up against Gunner's womb to try and stop him from bleeding profusely. His mind was racing a million miles an hour as he grabbed Gunner, who was passed out, turned him on his side, and let his seat back. Reaching for his phone, he called 9-1-1.

Gunner laid lifeless in Jamison's lap, barely breathing. Jamison held on to his brother like it was the last time he would ever have with him. Tears ran down his face down on to Gunner's cheek.

"It's gone be okay, Gunner. You can't die on me like dad did. I don't know what I would do without you."

Jamison had a devilish look on his face as he continued to talk to Gunner. He wasn't going to let Dave get away with what he had just done. All his life, Gunner protected him. He was determined to light everyone up that was involved with Gunner's shooting but, first, he had to make sure Gunner was going to be okay.

13

~ONE WEEK LATER~

As Kimberly drove the short distance from her house to Gunner's apartment, her mind ran a mile a minute. All she could think about was all the things her family had been going through within the last few months.

Kimberly thought when Gunner returned home from doing his jail sentence, everything would go back to normal and her family would be complete again. However, that wasn't nearly what happened to her family. Instead of everyone coming together and showing their love for each other, Gunner and Jamison were on the odds.

However, since their problems came to an end and Kelsi was now back home and in safe arms, Kimberly felt that their family would be whole again. That was only short lived though.

The moment Kimberly received the call that Gunner had been shot in the back, it was like her world turned upside down. She didn't know what to think or how to feel; all she knew was that she needed to pray that he made it out safe.

After spending seven hours in the hospital alongside her family, Kimberly was happy to hear that Gunner would make a full recovery. The bullet didn't do much damage, but the shock of the bullet caused him to pass out. Within the last week, Kimberly had spent a lot of time telling Jamison that this situation wasn't his fault. She also begged him to not go out and get revenge because her and their family couldn't take anymore.

Kimberly pulled up to Gunner's apartment complex and saw that his car was parked a few spaces up. Also, she noticed that Kelsi's coupe was parked next to his. Thinking that they all were in his apartment, she exited her car and went inside without thinking about calling or sending a text, letting him know she was here.

Once Kimberly approached the door, she knocked and waited for someone to answer the door. Within seconds she heard someone's voice from the other side of the door, which caused her to raise her eyebrow.

"Who is it?" the unfamiliar voice called out again, only this time sounding closer.

"Kimberly," she answered. She shifted her body weight to her right leg, as she placed her hand on her hip and waited for someone to open the door.

"One second."

Within seconds, the door slowly opened and there stood a brown skin female. Kimberly was taking aback by the women who opened the door for her because she knew nothing about who she was. When she spoke to her sisters when they first arrived to Gunner's apartment, they said nothing about someone else being here.

Not knowing who this chick was or where she came from, Kimberly glanced at the numbers that decorated the front door, making sure she was at the correct apartment. And, sure enough, she was.

"Um, who are you?" Kimberly asked with her eyebrow still raised. She hadn't even stepped a foot in the house because she was so thrown off.

"You plan on coming in or you going to stay standing at the door?"

"I plan on getting an answer, that's what I plan on doing."

"Oh, okay. Well, I have some food heating up in the microwave, so I'm going to handle that. Whenever you're ready to come in, you can do so," Toni said before she walked away and left the door open.

"I know this bitch lying," Kimberly said before taking a deep breath.

"Gunner and your sisters are on their way back as well!" Toni called out over her shoulder.

Kimberly walked in the apartment, closed the door behind her, and made sure it was locked. Once that was done, she placed her LV Purse on the nearby sofa and made her way into the kitchen area. Once she reached it, she saw that Toni in fact was removing food from the microwave. Kimberly said nothing but stood up against the wall and remained silence. Although she was silent, her eyes were trained on Toni the entire time.

"Toni."

"Excuse me?" Kimberly asked.

"You asked who am I, so I'm answering the question."

"Toni is your name and..." Kimberly asked as she slowed her words to trail off.

"And any other information you would like, you can get from Gunner," Toni responded with a small smile on her face. Toni wasn't trying to be smart or anything, but she truly didn't know the extent of her and Gunner's relationship, so she kept her answer to herself.

"That answer don't sit well with me. How did you and Gunner meet?" Kimberly continued to say while walking closer to the island that sat in the middle of the kitchen.

"Through my father," Toni answered, keeping her answer short and simple. She was uneasy about telling Kimberly that she was his connect because she didn't know what all she knew already. Plus, working in the drug game wasn't something she went bragging about.

"Y'all work together?" Kimberly questioned with a big smile on her face. From her facial expression alone, Toni could tell that Kimberly knew something, she just wasn't sure what all she knew.

"Yea, we do actually."

"Oh, I know who you are," Kimberly said before bursting out laughing.

"What is that supposed to mean?" Toni asked with her head tilted to the side and her left eyebrow raised.

"You were the female that had him blushing on the phone and smiling from ear to ear," Kimberly answered before pausing and pressing her lips together. Toni couldn't even respond because she was laughing so hard.

"Exactly, you know what time I'm talking about," Kimberly added.

"Yea, the day he was at your mother's house and your youngest sister was fighting him for his phone," Toni said, causing the two of them to laugh out loud.

"Sure was. All three of us tried to bank him for his phone but, by the time we got the phone, you had hung up."

"Okay, yes, that was me on the phone."

"So, if I asked who you were, why not just say his girl-friend?" Kimberly asked before tucking her lips in and tilting her head to the side.

"We aren't in a relationship," Toni answered before taking a bite of her food.

"Mhm okay! Have you met my other two sisters?"

"No, by the time I got here, they had already left."

"Wait... so, how did you get in here? I know my brother has better sense than to leave his door open."

"I used my key," Toni honestly answered while avoiding eye contact with Kimberly.

"But you... not his... girlfriend. Something sounds a little off to me," Kimberly questioned with a pause between her words. She was trying to understand the situation Gunner was in, but Toni wasn't making anything crystal clear.

"He gave me a key the day after he came home from the hospital."

"Rightttttttt. You know nothing that you saying is believable, right."

"You know what, from here on out, refer all questions to your brother. Allow him to make sense of the things he does," Toni said while laughing. Truthfully, she agreed with what Kimberly was saying; nothing she was telling Kimberly made any logical sense, but everything she was saying was the truth.

"Believe me, I will. Ain't no way you should have got a key before my sisters and me," Kimberly stated before the two of them continued to laugh.

"It feels so good to be able to shop until I drop," Kelsi said as she held all of her shopping bags in her hands and playfully danced around in a circle.

"Kelsi, shut up and walk across the street before I kick you in the ass," Jessica joked as she swung her bags in her directions.

"Chile, I'm in a good mood, shut your butt up," Kelsi playfully fussed as she bucked at Jessica. Jessica bucked back, causing Kelsi to run across the street.

Toni watched the interaction between the sisters in awe. The relationship between the Brown sisters was the relationship she wanted with her sister, Aries. Unfortunately, Aries wasn't like any of the Gunner sisters; she didn't have any ambitions and all she wanted to do was chase behind a man.

"Toni, you have any siblings?" Jessica asked after turning her attention to Toni while they walked across the street.

"Yes, I have a sister," Toni answered.

"That's it?" Kelsi asked, as if she was surprised.

"Unless my parents have some kids I don't know about then, yes, that's it."

"Good for you! If I didn't have all these damn sisters and brother, I wouldn't have to dye my grey hair black," Kimberly chimed in, causing Kelsi to kiss her teeth and roll her eyes.

"I just saying, Kelsi. Your ass stress me out the most."

"You ain't lying about that," Jessica added.

"First off, I don't even ask y'all for anything. I go to Gunner and Jamison for my needs," Kelsi objected as she placed her hand on her hip and stopped mid-stride in the middle of the street.

"You go to them for your financial needs, but come to us for everything else," Kimberly said.

"Food, clothes, shelter, hell, you even think we do hair and makeup for a living," Jessica cosigned.

"It's okay Kelsi. Gunner might not admit it, but he secretly likes when you come to him for things. He said it makes him feel like you're still the little baby he used to feed," Toni spoke with a smile on his face.

"At least one of my many siblings love me," Kelsi said as she continued to walk.

The four ladies continued to walk through the parking lot until they reached Toni's truck. They all drove together since they planned to go back Gunner's house right after. Everything about their outing was going well until they ran into Lakesha.

"Hey Lakesha!" Jessica called out, as Lakesha walked closer in their directions.

Unlike the past few months, when Lakesha would follow Gunner and Toni around the city, it was a coincidence that the two of them came face to face today. Lakesha thought of just saying hello and keep walking, but being presented with the chance to confront Toni for the first time seemed like a better idea.

"So, this the shit y'all on now?" Lakesha questioned as she spoke to Kimberly, Jessica, and Kelsi, but kept her eyes trained on Toni.

"Excuse me?" Kimberly asked as if she was stupid.

"Yea, what the hell is your issue?" Kelsi also questioned. She was taken back by the slick shit that was flying out of Lakesha's mouth.

"Gunner and I ended our relationship a short time ago, and y'all asses didn't waste no time to be buddy-buddy with his new bitch," Lakesha fussed, expressing her anger.

"Girl, go ahead with that dumb ass shit," Jessica said as she waved Lakesha off and rolled her eyes.

"Jessica, you know it's the fucking truth," Lakesha snapped as she finally removed her attention from Toni and turned to Jessica.

"Lakesha, you are out of line. You may be feeling some type of way or whatever is going on. However, regardless, you need to walk away and go about your business," Kimberly said as she took a step closer to her.

"All I have to say is, you think he may be yours but he not, believe me. He will be running back to me like he always does. You just a quick nut and comfortable shelter but, bitch, you could never be me, nor do the shit I have done for him."

"Sweety, you look like a fucking fool. The last thing I'm trying to do is be like you or anyone else. I'll be at my car waiting because I don't have time for this shit," Toni snapped before rolling her eyes and attempting to walk away.

"While you playing house with my man, make sure you can get everything from him that you can because trust and believe, when he comes back home, that shit is over with."

"Bitch, you broke as hell, shut the fuck up!" Toni yelled over her shoulder while laughing to herself.

"Bitch, keep talking shit, and I'll make sure that little boy you care for comes up missing by morning."

"Repeat that shit again," Toni snapped as she turned on her heels with her face scrunched up.

"You fucking heard me-" Lakesha began to fuss back but was cut off.

"Woah, woah, Lakesha, you really need to go ahead somewhere." Kimberly jumped between Toni and Lakesha and attempted to break them apart.

"Bitch, don't ever allow my nephew to come across your mentally ill ass mind. Say what you want about me, but mention him again and your fucking body will be swimming in the fucking ocean," Toni fussed through gritted teeth.

"Bitch, fuck his retarded looking ass." As soon as the words left Lakesha's mouth, Toni reached back and punched her right in the jaw.

Immediately, Lakesha grabbed the side of her face and was in a little shock that Toni would go as far as putting her hands on her. However, that didn't matter at this point, the damage was already done. Not wanting to go out like a punk, Lakesha reacted.

Lakesha quickly removed the small blade, which she held under her tongue, and attempted to slice Toni with it. Toni saw what was going on and immediately ducked, protecting herself from being cut. Lakesha continued to wave the small blade around, missing with every swing.

Toni knew that if she really put her hands on Lakesha, she would hurt her. In Toni's mind, anyone who used a weapon in a fist fight was really a bitch in her eyes. She had so much pent-up aggression stored inside that one hit would lead to Toni damaging Lakesha really bad. However, she wasn't about to allow anyone to step out of line.

Toni grabbed a hold of Lakesha's wrist and twisted her arm behind her back, forcing her to turn around in pain. Toni pushed her towards the ground, causing Lakesha to fall and hit her face.

As soon as Lakesha turned on her back, Toni snatched the gun from her waist and placed her foot on her neck. Lakesha couldn't move, even if she wanted to, and the gun pointed directly in her face didn't help the situation.

"Bitch, make another fucking move and I will peel your shit back right here," Toni snapped.

"Toni, chill out. She not worth it and people are starting to turn their attention to us," Jessica pleaded as she looked around at all the onlookers that began to gather around. In the perfect world, the sight of a gun would have caused people to run away but, shit, they were in the heart of Miami; people were used to seeing guns drawn on people during any time of the day.

"People are pulling out their phones, let's just walk away," Kimberly added.

"Only reason I'm going to let you live is because I rather you see Gunner and I live our best lives, you miserable bitch," Toni stated as she pressed down harder on Lakesha's throat.

Toni finally removed her foot and allowed Lakesha to catch her breath while she placed the gun back on her hip. Toni didn't bother to say anything else; instead, she grabbed her bags and continued to head to her car. She hated that she had to step out of character, but she had to do what was needed.

"Oh, Gunner got a crazy one on his hands," Kelsi said as they settled down in the truck.

14

———

"Kesha, seriously, what the fuck happened?" Mia questioned as she held the bag of ice to her best friend's jaw. The entire side of Lakesha's face was red and swollen from the punch that Toni delivered.

"I'm fine Mia," Lakesha tried to object as she rolled her eyes.

"No, the hell you're not. You just got into a damn fight with some bitch and now you sitting here like this. How the fuck did this shit happen in the first place?"

"I ran into Gunner's new bitch and some few choice words were exchanged between us. One thing led to another and some fists were thrown," Lakesha explained.

"Just like that?"

"Yup, just like that."

"What did Gunner have to say about any of this?" Mia asked.

"Fuck him! I haven't spoken to him since he came and got his shit from here," Lakesha snapped while getting upset.

"Wait, so if he wasn't there when you two started fighting, how did you know who she was?"

"She was with his bitch ass sisters. I can't even explain how they could be all buddy with her, knowing all the years I put in on this shit," Lakesha vented.

"Why can't you expect that? Their loyalty is with Gunner and Jamison, not the females they are dating."

"Yea, but that shit still hurt. I created a bond with all three of them and this was how they repay me. None of them bitches even called to check up on me. I spoke to Kimberly because I reached out to her, and that was it. I was like family to them, so hell yea I expect some type of support in the breakup," Lakesha explained how she was feeling deep down.

"That's not their place though Kesha, and that's what I'm trying to explain to you. You're expecting things from all the wrong people. If you needed someone to vent to, I'm a phone call away. If you need advice, then I'm sure your mother would have answered," Mia explained.

"You have a point, but-" Lakesha began to explain her point but was interrupted by the knocking on the front door.

Knock! Knock! Knock!

Although she wasn't expecting anyone to stop by, she stood up from where she was sitting on the floor and went to look through the peep hole. Seeing that the person on the other side of the door was her mother, she took a deep breath to brace herself for what she knew was coming before she opened the door.

"Oh, my god, baby girl, are you okay?" her mother asked with concern written all over her face.

"Yes mommy, yes, I'm okay," Lakesha said as she moved her head back from her mother's reach. Lakesha moved to the side, so her mother could walk in. As Vivian entered the house, her eyes never left Lakesha.

"Are you sure? Who is this person you got into a fight with?" Vivian continued to question as she overlooked her daughter's beautiful face. Her jaw was swollen, her eyes were red and swollen as well. Lakesha looked as if she hadn't slept in days, and the non-stop crying she was doing didn't help.

Vivian knew this all too well; Lakesha could lie and try to talk herself out of anything, but she wasn't fooling her mother not one bit. She knew her daughter wasn't taking her medicine and, at a time like this, when her emotions and hormones were all over the place, she needed them the most.

"No one. How do you even know that I got into a fight?"

"Gunner called and said something about you attacked a female at the mall," Vivian announced.

"Why are you even in contact with him?" Lakesha snapped way more aggressive than she should have.

"He contacted me to let me know what was going on with you. Hell, if he wouldn't have reached out, then you surely wouldn't have."

"Right, I wouldn't have because it's not serious enough to get you involved."

"The hell it is. If something bad would have happened to you or if you would have gotten locked up for assault, then it would have been me by your side. Mia, talk to your friend because, clearly, she has lost her mind," Vivian fussed as she felt herself getting upset.

Here she was trying to comfort her daughter and make sure she was okay, and she wanted to act ungrateful. Vivian stood up from the sofa she had just sat on and marched into the kitchen. She needed to take a moment and calm herself before she did something to Lakesha that Lakesha would regret.

"Kesha, chill out. I understand you're upset, but your mother is not the person to take it out on. She cares about your health and safety and wants nothing but the best for you," Mia said in a soft tone. She hated to see her best friend like this, especially over a man.

"I know... I'll be right back," Lakesha spoke back in a

defeated tone. With her head hung low, she followed her mother into the kitchen.

"Ma," she called out with tears in her eyes.

"Yes, Kesha."

"I'm sorry mommy. I'm way out of line."

"You're fine; I've just been so worried about you since you two broke up. I'm scared you're going to do something you regret," Vivian admitted as she looked her daughter directly in the eyes.

"I really love him to death mommy, I swear," Lakesha cried out.

"That's the scary part. Have you been taking your medicine?"

Lakesha didn't bother to answer; instead, she dropped her head and began to loudly sob. Lakesha knew what her mother was going to say and, in this moment, she knew everything she would say was going to be correct. Lakesha needed to get on some type of treatment for her Bipolar Disorder, but just taking her medicine was not going to fix her issues. She needed professional help; however, she didn't have the willpower to seek it on her own.

"Lakesha, you need to get help. The things you have been doing is not healthy. You can't love anyone else if you don't love yourself, and not taking care of your health shows your lack of self-love," Vivian explained, as she walked over to her daughter and wrapped her arms around her.

"Gunner did everything for me; he even provided a roof over my head when he was in jail. Without him, I have nothing; I don't even have a reason to live," Lakesha continued to sob.

"With or without Gunner, you still have a life to live, and family who still loves you! You have a hell of a lot to be here on earth for, and I don't want to hear otherwise. The first thing you need to do is check into an impatient care facility, get back on track with your meds, and get your life back right."

"I know mommy, I know. It's just so hard."

"I understand Kesha. In the morning, I am going to make some phone calls, so we can see about some inpatient treatment. However, in the meantime, you are coming home with me," Vivian explained as she and Lakesha rocked back and forth.

15

"I still can't believe that you're gone, cousin. It's really fucking me up that they took you away from me, when I needed you the most. We talked about taking over the entire fucking Florida; now, I have to do this shit on my own," Dave cried as he kneeled down in the wet dirt in front of Cornell's tombstone.

Since the funeral, Dave had been coming to the burial site everyday faithfully. He would come just to cry in peace. He was still devasted by the death of Cornell, and he was beating himself up that the killer was still on the loose. With today's visit, he wanted to ensure Cornell that he was going to fulfill every promise he made to him. However, unlike the other times Dave came here, this time, he wasn't alone.

"A plan not written down is just an idea," Jamison said, startling Dave.

"What the fuck!" Dave yelled as he jumped up and turned to face Jamison.

Jamison had followed Dave to the burial spot. He could have shot up his car or sent a bullet through his head while he was walking but, instead, Jamison wanted to make this personal. He didn't want Dave's mind to wonder with who killed him; instead, he wanted to prove a point, to not fuck with his family.

"You don't look happy to see me at all," Jamison said, pretending to be offended.

"Fuck you Jamison! You need to fucking go man! I'm not in the mood for no shit," Dave fussed.

Up until now, Dave was using Jamison to get closer to his brother. He never told Jamison that he knew Gunner was responsible; instead, he acted as if he knew nothing. When Dave did ask about that night, he told Dave that he never made it to the meeting spot.

Jamison never thought twice about Dave being a snake because he wasn't aware that the two of them were family. As long as he knew Cornell, he never spoke of Dave. However, after doing research, Jamison learned otherwise.

"I heard you was looking for me, Dave. I'm not that hard to find though, so I'm a little confused," Jamison said as he scratched the side of his head.

"You damn right, you not hard to find. I wasn't looking for you; I was looking for the nigga that killed my cousin."

"So, you ride down on us and shoot up the car?" Jamison questioned. He wanted Dave to admit that he was responsible and not hide his hand like a bitch.

"If that's what it takes to catch a nigga slipping, then so be it," Dave snapped.

"See, that's were your wrong. We stay ready, so we never have to get ready. Your bitch ass could never catch any of us slipping."

"You don't even like that nigga, now you want the best brother of the fucking year award. Kiss my ass. I'm just trying to do what you too pussy to do on your own."

"That's where you wrong. We family, brothers to be exact,

we fuss and fight like anyone else. However, I will be damned if I allow anyone to hurt him," Jamison fussed.

"Right, just like I'm not allowing my cousin to go out like that," Dave spat as he snatched the gun from his hip.

Being on his p's and q's, Jamison saw the move Dave was about to make before he actually made it, causing him to snatch his 9mm off his hip. They both let off shots seconds from one another. Jamison followed behind his one shot and let of an additional three. Jamison's bullets ripped through Dave's shoulder, causing his arm to fly upward and his aim to be off. As Dave's arm flew in the air, his gun flew out of his hand.

"Don't ever fucking disrespect me or my fucking family again. You thought you were doing something good by trying to work undercover, but everything comes to the light eventually. You can't play a mother fucker who learned the game from a well-respected OG."

"Bitch, fuck you!" Dave spat before spitting in Jamison's face.

With an evil laugh, Jamison removed the spit off the side of his face before raising his gun and striking him across the face with the end of it. Due to the hard hit, Dave immediately spit out two of his teeth. With his mouth filling with blood, Jamison struck him two more times.

"Since you want to follow Cornell's footsteps so much, you can burn in hell with his ass," Jamison snapped before raising his gun and sending a shot through Dave's skull. He didn't allow Dave to say any last words because truthfully, anything he said from this point wouldn't have meant anything to him.

Jamison watched as Dave's body hit the ground and his head bounced off the tombstone. Without any remorse, Jamison turned on his heels and walked over to his car. He left just as quietly as he came.

"How is your food?" Jamison asked as he awkwardly sat across from his wife.

The two of them had been eating dinner for the past hour and a half and had only spoken a matter of a few words. Jamison wanted so bad to talk to his wife and make matters between them better, but he didn't know how to start the conversation.

"It's pretty good. Last time we came here, the food was better though," Amber admitted as she moved her mash potatoes around her plate with her fork.

"I can tell. You barely even touched your steak," Jamison acknowledged.

"Truthfully, I'm not that hungry. I ate a big lunch at work today."

"Oh..." Jamison said while allowing his words to trail off.

"How is your food?" Amber asked.

"My food is actually really good. You want to try some?"

"No, I'm good. The Salmon looks nicely seasoned though."

"Yea, it is."

"That's good."

"I'll just get right to it... I wanted you and I to get out the house and enjoy each other's company. Also, so we can discuss the relationship and anything else we have going on," Jamison said after being tired of the small talk.

"I'm listening."

"Well, you know I love you."

"No, I don't. What I know is that your mouth tells me that you love me, but the actions you display show a completely different thing," Amber interrupting while cutting his words short.

"I know my actions have been off and that's fucked up on my part. I'm willing to do anything that's needed of me, so I can fix my mistakes. I just want to make sure I'm not wasting my time," Jamison admitted to his wife.

"But, what if your actions are something I can't look past?"

"Then, I guess I will have to deal with it. If you choose to end the relationship and move on, then I will have to move on and allow you to seek your own happiness."

"Jamison, to be perfectly honest with you, I don't know what I want to do. One minute, I wake up and I want to make our relationship work. Then, there are other times when I think about moving on because I believe I would never trust you again," Amber admitted. She wasn't going to lie to him or to herself; she was confused on what she wanted to do.

"From this moment forward, all I want is for you to be happy. I'm praying that I could be the reason behind the happiness, but I understand that things take time," Jamison also admitted. For once, he was acknowledging that he fucked up and he was taking responsibility of his actions.

"I hear all of that Jamison, but we are at the point where words don't mean anything, only actions. And even then, I need to see long term change. I don't want you to change for a few months, just so I can be blinded by love, then you revert back to the same ways that put us in the situation."

"I know. It's just hard dealing with everything. I let the power, money, and the titles change the person I was. I hurt so many people in the process, and I'm doing everything I can to right my wrongs. I know for a fact my father is looking down at me in disgust, and that's what upset me the most," Jamison said as he fought back tears.

"You need to get back to your old self. When we first got married, you were everything I wanted in a man. You just need to go back to the man you once were. You're not a bad person; you just lost sight of what was important."

"I know, and I'm sorry."

"What's done is done. We can't change the past, all we can

do is create a better future," Amber said with a reassuring smile.

"Just promise me one thing."

"And what is that?"

"That no matter where our relationship goes from here, you never keep my child away from me," Jamison said while looking her directly in the eyes.

"I'm actually offended that you think I would keep her away. You may have been a piece of shit husband and person, but I would never down talk the love you have for our child. As long as you want to be in her life, you will be. But, please understand that I'm not forcing her on anyone."

"And I wouldn't ask you to," Jamison said before dropping the conversation.

For the remainder of the night, Jamison and Amber reminisced on their old memories together. Times like this was what Amber cherished. She knew sides of Jamison that no one else thought existed. He wasn't the man the streets created, and she was pleased to hear him acknowledge that he needed to change. The dinner the two of them had left Amber even more confused than she was previously was.

EPILOGUE

~18 MONTHS LATER~

"Surprise!" Everyone yelled in unison as Gunner entered the back yard of his new home.

Today was his birthday, and what he thought was going to be a chill day had turned into a full-on cookout. Jamison and he had just come back from wasting time in the mall.

"Nigga, you knew all about this shit, didn't you?" Gunner turned to Jamison and asked him with a big smile spread across his face.

"Toni told me if I didn't do as she said, she was going to stab me," Jamison admitted as he shrugged his shoulder and laughed. Gunner playfully pushed him away, as Toni and his sister approached them.

"Happy birthday big brother," Kelsi said as she hugged Gunner,

"Happy birthday Gunner," Jessica added.

"Happy Birthday big head," Kimberly also added.

"Thanks y'all," Gunner responded as he gave each one of his sisters a hug.

"Happy birthday baby," Toni said as she walked into his

awaiting arms.

"Thank you so much baby!" Gunner said before placing his lips on Toni's. The two of them stood in the middle of the backyard surrounding by friends and family and kissed on one another. Although people were around, it was like they were in their own little world.

"Okay, you two, don't nobody want to see all of that," Maria playfully fussed as she waved the two of them off.

"Ma, you a hater, that's all that is."

"I'm not hating on anything. Now, shut your mouth and take a picture."

"How you going to talk trash and want me to do something for you?"

"Easy, because I'm the parent," Maria fussed as she tilted her head to the side and waited for him to say something in response. Once Gunner laughed without hitting her with a response, she held her phone up and snapped a picture of him and a smiling Toni.

"Now, let's eat!" Gunner announced, as she rubbed on his stomach.

"Yea, you can say that again," Toni co-signed. Gunner wrapped his arm around her waist and walked in the direction of where the food was held.

In the past eighteen months, the relationship between Toni and Gunner had grown tremendously. They decided to take the relationship slow, but the love they had for one another was still growing.

Granted, they weren't living together, but they had keys to each other's house. Their family and friends were aware of the relationship and was pleased that they were making each other happy. They weren't hiding one another; hell, if anything, they were flaunting each other around the city. But, most importantly, they were happy and content with what they had going on.

Gunner hadn't been this happy in a long time. To be surrounded by nothing but family and close friends on such a special day was everything to him. For once since his father's death, he felt whole again. He didn't have to stress about how to make money because he was making a lot of it now. But, most importantly, he didn't have to question Jamison's every move.

Speaking of Jamison, things for him had changed as well. His marriage was still on the rocks but, with Amber now moved out of their home and into a two bedroom condo, Jamison really had to come to grips with the reality he was facing.

Jamison and Amber may have still been legally married but, emotionally, mentally, and physically, Amber was somewhere else. Amber needed space away from Jamison to really think about what it was that she wanted. Being in the home with Jamison was clouding her mind because he was doing and saying everything he felt he needed to do to win his wife back.

Only, she didn't think that moving out of the house she shared with her husband and being away from him would push her into the arms of another man. Yes, that man was Bruce. He made her feel special, like she was the only female in the world to him. She didn't have to worry about other females hanging on to him, nor did she have to worry about him disrespecting her. He took every action needed to treat her like the queen she was.

But, most importantly, she didn't have to worry about him not coming home at night, or seeing his face flash across the news channel. For once, she was dealing with a normal man, with a normal job. For once, she felt like a normal girl again. She didn't have to pretend to be a ride or die chick any more. Granted, at one point the thrill excited her, but now she was older, much wiser, and she had someone she had to protect, her daughter

Although the marriage was coming to an end, Jamison still had his daughter 4 days out of the week and face-time with her on the days she was with her mother. True indeed, Amber stayed true to her word and never kept Jamie away from her father, and that was all that Jamison could ask for. Knowing his fuck ups, he respected Amber's movements and didn't make it hard for her to move on. Deep down he was hurt, but he couldn't blame anyone but himself.

"Let me holla at you for a second Gunner," Latrell said to Gunner once he was done making his plate of food.

"Let's go over here," Gunner said as he nodded his head towards the side of the house. The two of them walked over to the side where they were alone by themselves.

"What's up?" Gunner said.

"I did what you asked me to do," Latrell said.

"How she doing?"

Gunner asked Latrell to keep tabs on Lakesha. For one, he wanted to know how she was doing because he wanted to protect himself and his family. He wasn't sure what she capable of doing, but also, he cared because he still had love for her. She may have done him dirty and he wasn't in love with her anymore, but he still had love for her in his heart.

"From what I hear, she good for the most part. My little birdie from Pennsylvania told me that she out the facility and back on common grounds," Latrell informed.

"Common grounds meaning back in MIA?" Gunner asked for clarification.

"Yea. I put my ear to the streets though and she staying with her mother."

"I'll call her mother and see what's up with that," Gunner said before kissing his teeth and nodding his head up and down.

"Done already."

"Well, shit, with you on everything, I can lay back, kick my feet up, and chill," Gunner joked.

"Nah, not at all. I just wanted to check in case I needed to put a bullet in her head," Latrell said with a shrug of the shoulders.

"I feel you. What her mother talking about?"

"Nothing. Her mother agreed to keep her away from you and your family. I also made sure moms knew that if Lakesha did anything stupid, then that would be their life," Latrell informed, causing Gunner eyes to grow big.

Vivian was always nice and caring to Gunner, so he would have never threatened that woman's life. Regardless, if the threat would keep Lakesha in line, that's all that mattered to him.

"Your ass sure can be evil when you want to," Gunner said, causing Latrell to give an evil and sneaky laugh.

"Sorry to interrupt guys but, Gunner, someone wants to see you," Toni said as she approached the guys.

"You good sis."

"Who wants to see me that I haven't already seen?" Gunner questioned.

"Just follow me," Toni said as she grabbed a handful of his shirt and led him to where everyone else was.

Gunner was so busy trying to stuff his face that his eyes were trained on his plate and not on who was standing before him. As soon as he looked up, a big smile spread across his face. Toni grabbed the plate from his hands and allowed her father and Gunner to properly hug one another.

"They finally let your ass up out the big house?" Gunner asked after the two of them let each other go.

"You know they couldn't hold a real nigga down for long, young blood," Santana said.

Toni stood to the side and watched in awe as Santana and Gunner talked. In this moment, for her, life was complete. She had her man, her father was home and, most importantly, she was living a peaceful life. She couldn't have asked for anything better.

THE END!!

MORE READS BY SHYKEL W

Loyal to No Other
Loyal to No Other 2
Her Sweet Addiction
She Want That Thug Lovin'
She Want That Thug Lovin' 2
She Want That Thug Lovin' 3
A Thug Valentine In Baltimore: A Hood Love Story
Issa Hood love Story: Dallas & Dinero
Fallin For An A-Town Savage

CONNECT WITH SHYKEL W. ON SOCIAL MEDIA:

FACEBOOK: SHYKEL WILLIAMS

Instagram: *Author_ShykelW*
Email: *Authorshykelw@gmail.com*

MORE READS BY LA'QUANA JONES

California Hood Luv 1
California Hood Luv 2
Cali Black and Kisha 1
Cali Black and Kisha2
Fallin' For a Sacramento Boss
Issa Hood Love Story: Jacquelyn & Finesse

CONNECT WITH LA'QUANA JONES ON SOCIAL MEDIA:

FACEBOOK: AUTHOR.LAQUANA JONES

Twitter: @Laquanasheart
Instagram: Laquanas_World
Email: **Laquanasheart1@gmail.com**

www.ingramcontent.com/pod-product-compliance
Lightning Source LLC
Chambersburg PA
CBHW022140150726
47992CB00002B/690